Sleep is a Beautiful Colour

A collection of flash-fictions

Edited by
Santino Prinzi and Meg Pokrass

A National Flash-Fiction Day and Gumbo Press publication

First Published 2017 by National Flash-Fiction Day
in association with Gumbo Press

National Flash-Fiction Day
18 Caxton Avenue
Bitterne
Southampton
SO19 5LJ
www.nationalflashfictionday.co.uk

A CIP Catalogue record for this book
is available from the British Library

ISBN 978-1547192618

To You:
Keep Reading,
Keep Writing,
Keep Going.

Contents

National Flash-Fiction Day 2017
Micro-Fiction Competition Winners

Foreword

You're holding the sixth anthology in celebration of National Flash-Fiction Day, but we believe that this anthology represents so much more than that.

This year we decided on the theme 'Life As You Know It'. There's always a duality present when selecting a theme; we want something specific enough to give the anthology a focus, but broad enough to allow as many different stories as possible. We chose this theme because we wanted to create an empowering challenge for our authors. We wanted authors to create flash-fictions with voices that demand to be heard, to pen stories that show the world as only they or their characters know it, and to invite readers to see the world as they've never seen it before.

More of you than ever rose to the challenge: we had nearly 600 submissions, and for the first time ever, anthology submissions exceeded our micro-fiction competition submissions. You didn't make it easy for us, and the range of submissions proves that flash-fiction is a form that continues to grow not only in popularity, but in quality. This anthology showcases flashes that grasped us tightly and refused to let go, flashes that opened our eyes to what remained unseen, and flashes that kept us awake at night.

With each anthology we produce, we seek to include commissioned stories from some of the world's finest flash-fiction writers – this year is no exception. In addition, and in keeping with tradition, we've included the ten winners of our micro-fiction competition. The selected title—taken from Helen Rye's hilarious and touching story—encapsulates the vividness of each of the lives in these flash-fictions. From the first story to the last, you will be captivated.

As always, these anthologies don't materialise from the ether. Thanks must go out to all of the writers who support NFFD every year, to those who work behind the scene and work so hard to make this all happen. We also want to thank and welcome those who have just joined the party. NFFD continues to grow, as does the wider community of flash-fiction writers, and we want to thank you all for your support, your kindness, and, most importantly, your stories.

As beautiful a colour sleep may be, we must warn you that you're not about to doze off. Get comfortable, and prepare to see life as you know it irrevocably altered.

Santino Prinzi & Meg Pokrass
Editors
June 2017

A Sky Full of Ghosts

Robert Scotellaro

It's before my first cup of coffee that she declares she's becoming a Buddhist.

"You mean that guy with the fat belly?"

"That's Chinese. I'm thinking Tibetan."

"Wow." There's still crud in my eyes and the cat hasn't been fed yet. It's got a small bell on its collar, and when it wants attention, it scratches like crazy, and the little bell jingles. It's jingling.

"I mean, what is heaven anyway, but a sky full of ghosts," she tells me. "Might as well hook up with a religion that believes in second chances. See if I can get it right next time around."

"What if you come back as a flea on a rat's ass?"

"Or a world-renowned opera singer," she says.

"I thought you hated opera."

"That's not the point. I'd like it *then*."

"What about being on Peaches? Just one of the crowd on Peaches?"

"*What?*"

"A flea on Peaches, dodging all those claws."

"Would you stop it with the flea thing. I'm thinking big. You ought to try it sometime."

"Okay, *Big*," I say, and pour a cup.

She stirs her coffee over and over like she's churning butter. I try to picture her somewhere in Italy singing opera. She's wearing a blonde wig with long braids and is across from this tall chubby guy in a helmet with horns on the side of it. He's got a beard and they're taking turns singing very loud (in a good way) and the audience loves it. I even see her in her dressing room, later, taking off her make-up. She looks happy. I think to tell her. But figure, it's too late for that.

There's sunlight pouring in and she squints, but doesn't move out of it. We sit across from each other, sipping, staring off and it's very quiet. Except for Peaches' bell, which is pretty damn loud now.

Molly and the Toe-rag

Catherine Edmunds

So we're in the bar and O'Keefe leans in and says, 'We've never really been close.'

'What, you and Molly? Try pulling the other one.'

Molly's my sister, O'Keefe's the toe-rag she's been shacked up with for the last five years. When I called round earlier, their kid tried to swipe the pages of my paperback. That's what happens when you're brought up on an iPad. I told Molly what I thought, and she told me to fuck off.

'There's a third person in this marriage,' she said, 'and it's bloody you. Piss off, Jimmy, and let us be.'

Thing is, I have no problem with who she loves, just how she's loved back, and O'Keefe is clearly trying to weasel himself out of this relationship. I look round the bar, expecting to see some teenager with too much slap ogling him, but the place is empty. We drink up and head out. Kick-off's in a few minutes.

O'Keefe doesn't speak. He has his hands in his pockets and his head down. He's marching quickly which isn't like him at all.

At one-nil he says, 'I'm pissing blood.'

'Go see the quack.'

'I did. It's bad.'

Fuck. I don't have words for this sort of thing.

'Have you told Molly?'

'Tried to. Said I'd seen the doc about *down there* and she pulled down me pants and laughed, said that's the biggest boil on your arse yet, can I lance it for yer? So I slept in the spare.

Couldn't stop her laughing. She woke up Rory with her laughing and he was crying and she was laughing and fuck it, how was I supposed to say anything?'

Half time. Does he want a pie? No. Neither do I. Appetite gone. Damn you to hell, O'Keefe. You do not do this to my sister.

And then he says it again, slowly and sadly. 'We've never really been close.'

If we were lasses I suppose I'd put an arm round his shoulder, and maybe we'd have a little cry.

Second half starts and it's beautiful, it's poetry, it's as if they know.

We walk home and O'Keefe is shining.

Molly is out the back kicking a ball around with the kid. I grab O'Keefe and give him a very, very swift hug.

I leave before Molly sees us. Damn you, O'Keefe. I'm not crying.

Soup Stone

Simon Sylvester

It was a stone, and no more than a stone — a smooth, round pebble gathered from St. Bees on the day of my second birthday. It was only a stupid rock, but my mother held an unwavering belief that it soaked up the flavours of every soup she made. She was convinced that those old flavours quietly seeped out of the stone, and so improved the taste. Whenever she cooked a soup, it was the first thing that went into the pot.

Obviously I knew this was impossible, though no amount of argument could ever change her mind. It drove me crazy. That smug plop as she dropped it into the stock — the scrape of it stirring around the bottom of the pan. It was like a soup ghost, haunting the pots.

After my mother died, I found the soup stone at the back of the drawer of kitchen utensils. I didn't think twice before tossing it into the garden, glad to be rid of the ridiculous thing.

A month or so later, I made soup. I followed the recipe exactly, but it didn't taste quite right. I mean, it didn't taste particularly bad. It wasn't bland or over-seasoned or anything like that — it simply wasn't right. I couldn't figure out the problem until Jim piped up.

'Oh, it's fine, love,' he said, wiping soup out of his beard. 'It's not bad at all.' Then his face went dreamy. 'Hey,' he said. 'Do you remember your Mum's leek soup? That really made the leeks sing, didn't it?'

A squirmy feeling crawled in the pit of my stomach. The next day I made a minestrone, just to see.

'It's lovely,' said Jim, politely. 'It's very nice.'

'Hmm. Remember Mum's pasta bean soup?'

His gaze went faraway.

'Sometimes, when I'm at work,' he said, 'I stop to think about that soup.'

I dropped my spoon and raced back to Mum's house. I sifted the lawn with my fingers, and then again, until the new owners threatened to call the police, but I couldn't find the soup stone. It was gone, it was gone, and I could almost hear her voice in my head.

It's only a daft rock, remember?

The next day, at lunchtime, as I was grating carrots and rinsing lentils, I began to cry. I wept for my mother, and wept for her stupid soup stone too. And then, for a long time, I stopped making soup.

But you're almost two years old. I'm almost ready to cook again. But first, we'll do something for your birthday. We'll go to St. Bees, where pebbles tumble circles in the surf, and we'll search amongst the stones until we find one that remembers my mother.

And then, when we come home, I'll make you a soup.

The Quick and the Dead

Sandra Arnold

A poster at the intersection warns: *You're a long time dead. So what's the hurry?* Last week it was: *The Quick ARE the Dead.* The windscreen wipers squeak and scrape across the glass. She drums her fingers on the dashboard and waits for the lights to turn green. People scutter along the pavement, heads bent under black umbrellas. She stares at the lights. Red. The only spot of colour in this godforsaken morning. Rain sheets from the pewter sky and ricochets off the road like bullets on metal. If it doesn't let up by the time she heads home tonight all the fords will be flooded, same as last year. No. Not the same as last year. Nothing is the same as last year. But don't go there. Not before class. Focus on the rain. The scurrying people. The blue Mazda in front.

Watch the woman in the blue Mazda applying her lipstick in the rear-view mirror. Watch the children in the school bus pressing their faces against the back window, sticking their tongues out. Think about the essays she marked last night. Listen to the radio. Afghanis are throwing bombs at American soldiers, but President Bush reassures the American People and the Free World that he is closing in on Bin Laden. Someone says something about a build-up to the first anniversary of September 11. *In the hospital waiting room she watches the twin towers implode. The oncologist wipes his forehead with the back of his arm: "Extremely rare. Almost unheard of in your daughter's age group. In effect her appendix exploded."*

The lights turn green. The children in the bus give the finger. The Mazda woman applies blusher. The man in the van in the next lane picks his nose. WE'RE WELL HUNG!! the writing on the side of his van proclaims. Window frames. Door frames.

'The surgeons have cut out a lot of those secondary tumours, but of course some are so small at this stage they can't be seen yet with the naked eye.'

This stage.

Yet.

"…so if Bush thinks that blasting a few Al Qaeda cells will eliminate terrorism he is very much mistaken. For every cell destroyed, hundreds more will grow and spread…"

'We'll blast them with chemotherapy, of course, However…'

Breathe. Keep breathing.

Get a mooooove on! How many times does this light have to turn green before anybody bloody mooooves? Has the whole world stopped dead in its tracks?

The bus slowly drifts forward. The woman in the blue Mazda doesn't notice the lights changing and puts the finishing touches to her eye-liner. Drivers tap their horns. The bus accelerates. The Mazda woman fluffs out her hair and turns left. The well-hung van man stops drilling his nose and turns right. The bold black letters of the ice rink ad on the back of the bus rear up.

Iridescence

Heather McQuillan

Florian arranged the peacock feather in the can of Smirnoff Ice, just so, then leaned back to see me better, his hands forming a headrest. "Home does your head in!"

It hurt when I grinned but Florian's laugh was like no other. It started as a tinkle of piss onto hot corrugated iron and built to a crescendo of smoky-lung cackling. It was the best laugh in the world and the best thing was, that even if the others never seen the joke, they laughed too, just because it were him.

The next morning I stashed the feather in my backpack. It was a dumb thing to do, the stem snapped and the edges frayed, but each morning, wherever I woke, I twirled it to let the sun catch each frond of the shimmering green-blue eye.

Florian wore clothes he nicked out The Sallies' bins. He'd put things together you'd never think would work and model them for us. He was so beautiful it made your eyes water. I fell in love with him but I weren't his type. He'd set his sights way too high on some guy who promised him the earth. We're all just looking for love.

His name wasn't really Florian. I'd guessed that. It were too perfect. When soup-kitchen-lady Janine, all soft floury hands and heart of milky kindness, asked if we'd heard the terrible news about Hayden we just stared at our filthy sneakers. Then she said, "He was the one with pink tips on his hair and, you know, that gorgeous walk, I saw him with you lot—and that laugh!"

Then we knew.

The peacock feather, he got that from outside The Sallies

too. I downed a can of Smirnoff in his honour and stuck the tattered feather in it, just so. My eye was healed up by then. The blue bruising was faded to yellow.

Close Encounters

James Coffey

Life is a habit. I read that somewhere. Today is my husband Robert's birthday and we are having a family dinner and I am thinking about the world spinning on its axis in the opposite direction and I am wondering if the sun would rise in the West and set in the East and if the Gulf Stream would flow the other way.

Laurence, my nephew, shouts, "Look what Auntie Jean's done."

I have sculpted my mash like a mountain. Nobody speaks.

"Didn't somebody do that in a film?" Robert says as he kicks my foot. He says I have been like a zombie recently.

The trick is to try to liberate each day from the monotony of days. Robert proclaims that I cook a wonderful roast dinner. His mother agrees. What if the Gulf Stream did flow in the opposite direction, would the Trade Winds blow the other way? We all end up subsumed in drudgery. Did somebody say that?

"I know how it is," says Carol, Robert's sister. "You cook a meal and completely lose your own appetite. Strange isn't it?"

"What was that film?" Robert.

"I should have given you a hand," Lynn, Robert's mother.

"We'll do the washing up, won't we Lynn?" says Jack, Robert's Dad.

"Don't be silly," I say.

"It was *Close Encounters*," Philip, Carol's husband.

Robert goes to the kitchen for wine. Michael, Robert's brother caresses my foot with his. Michael thinks that one foolish moment at another family celebration years before retains a promise of fulfilment. I remove my foot and give him a hostile look. He responds with a conspiratorial smile.

I continue sculpting mash. If the trade winds did blow the other way would the history of colonisation be reversed? Would New York be in the eastern hemisphere, would the Aztecs still rule in Mexico?

"What was the actor's name? Richard something or other?" Philip asks.

"Dreyfuss," says Jack.

"Can't we talk about something else?" Lynn asks.

"If Jean doesn't have an appetite so what?" Michael says.

"I don't understand," says Jack.

"Richard Dreyfuss was obsessing about his mash, you know, obsessing," Lynne hisses. Jack shakes his head.

I'll do that writing course. I'll have my hair cut short and coloured blonde. I'll get a tattoo.

"There's a place nearby where people swim naked in the sea on Christmas Day," I announce. "We should do it too. Swim naked in the sea."

"Count me in," says Michael and winks.

Then there is silence. I take my plate to the kitchen and start to clear away.

When everybody has left Robert says I behaved dreadfully and that he will sleep in the spare bedroom.

I look at the stars and beyond them to the unknowingness of things and wonder if we might ever see the world anew, and if I might ever come to know myself, and I wonder if buffalo would still roam the Atlantic shore and if the City on a Hill would have been in Ulan Bator.

Aino Yehudi

Victoria Richards

I know it is over the day you refuse to share wine with me, because I am dirty.

"Impure," you call me, caught on a loop, too flustered by the constraints of translation to soften the blow. "Mevushal?" you ask of the bottle, a Hebrew word I've never heard. I roll it around my mouth like Merlot, tasting the syllables. "Me-vu-shal." I wait, looking at you the way I'd look at a child explaining a dream. I take quiet notes of your face: complexion, slightly reddened; the spatter of freckles across the bridge of your nose flushed dark and uneven; your eyes, a startled hazel-green. You use your hands more when you're embarrassed. You are waving them at me now, at the waitress, out to the side of you and above your head, like a mime struggling to convey some small horror. I can barely hear you. The words sound to me like they would to a deep-sea diver, echoes from the surface, metres away.

"Impure," I parrot, testing it out. The word tastes sour on my tongue. I feel a strange, detached sorrow for the poor Israeli waitress, who is growing increasingly confused as you attempt to convey the reasons we can't both drink from the same bottle. "Jewish," you say slowly in English, pointing at your heart. "Not." That second word belongs to me. I'm not kosher, and neither is the wine. It is simple, I suppose. Only to me, it isn't.

I look out through the window of the tiny restaurant. It is yellow outside, dusty. Men hurry past in tall, bearskin hats and thick, black coats, despite the Middle Eastern heat. You are used to the scorching midday sun. It's been months since you swapped London for Jerusalem, secularism for careful observance.

After, we walk in silence through the strange, closeted neighbourhood of Mea She'arim. "Please do not pass through our neighbourhood in immodest clothes," a sign screams in black and white. Beneath, in red: "Modest clothes include closed blouse, with long sleeves, long skirt – no trousers, no tight-fitting clothes." My long skirt tickles the tops of my feet. I am sweating beneath the shirt covering me from collarbone to cuff. I tug at the delicate, silver-threaded shawl around my shoulders, my only souvenir from the shuk. It falls to the floor, crumpled. I walk away before I can miss it.

At the gate leaving the Old City I pause, reaching down to scratch the soft inside of my ankle. There's a small black star, tattooed there. You know, because you've got one too, a permanent marker of our 15-year friendship. What happens when a star dies? If it's really big, it has so much mass that after the helium is all used up, it still has enough carbon to fuse it into heavy elements like iron. When the core turns to iron, it no longer burns. Will we still burn, after this? And if so, for how long?

DIY

Kevlin Henney

She decided to do it herself.

There were, of course, good — very good — reasons she shouldn't. Yes, it was a decision, but no, it was not obviously a good one. Obviously. But she felt she had no choice.

She was up early. Last night she lay awake in the skew-walled attic darkness, drumming rain and realisation that much as she wanted it, if she didn't do it, it wouldn't happen. Grandma and Grandpa were always delaying — always putting things off until next week, next month, next birthday — always dithering, always in the process of deciding but never deciding. Always and never. Nothing ever happened, nothing ever started.

If she started doing it and started messing it up — which she probably would do, because she was good at doing that, so Mum and Dad used to say — it was more likely Grandpa or Grandma would step in to help, step up to fix things and make things right — which they probably would do, because they were good at doing that.

She finished her cereal and juice, putting the bowl, spoon and glass aside in readiness for second breakfast. It was still dark as she went outside.

Splish. Splash. Drop. The room was going to be purple — that was decided — but how did she make purple again? She'd done it at school, but that was primary school. The world of secondary was bigger and heavier and less colourful, less filled with useful things, more filled with numbers and words and homework. In the sharp filament light the shelves in Grandpa's shed gave all kinds of suggestions. She followed each one, up and down the ladder in turn. Reds and blues — dark and light — milky cream, a dash of grass green, a moment of yellow.

It was veering towards unruly brown — definitely not the colour for a tweenager's room. Reclaimed and cracked, encrusted and undusted within, rain-streaked without, the shed window framed a dawn-silhouette of the house containing only the kitchen light. Still no one up. Still time to start. And restart.

New bucket. New paints — just red and blue, just the two, simple and primary. That was it. She mixed it with the trowel from Mum and Dad's house — her old house — before hobbling back, a magenta cookie trail following her from shed to kitchen across rain-clean grass.

If this was to be her room — and Grandma and Grandpa were to be Mum and Dad now Mum and Dad were gone — she wanted the room to be hers.

Splish, splash, drop, up the stairs, past the iron bath on the landing, up the ladder to the attic. Back down when she realised she'd forgotten to pick up a brush. Time was short — she had to start soon — and the shed too far — she might return to find Grandma and Grandpa awake.

She caught sight of the toilet brush through the door on the landing. Nothing a good rinse and a dose of red–blue–purple paint couldn't fix.

She would make this work.

Rehabilitation

Sophia Holme

About thirty years ago, summer was dying and I was working a mishmash of neighbourhood jobs—walking dogs, watering plants, moving furniture, mowing lawns. Domestic, physical jobs. Plus a taco truck shift.

I'd quit college after an incident involving a friend and a needle made it hard to work or sleep or give a shit, and now everyday a bit of grit or gravel would find its way into my mouth, and I'd grind it between my teeth while I worked.

Dogs began acting strangely. Like there was thunder in their heads. They would duck and pant, whimper. Sometimes they would be fine for half the walk then, suddenly cower. A few were fainters.

I remember carrying this Staffy home in my arms. Telling the owner—I still see her freckled nose and sparse bangs, short legs in short shorts—to call me again with a receipt from the vet.

That dog, slobbery, white, hair so short he looked bald. Wrinkled ears flat back, piss-coloured eyes worried.

That weekend he bit her. Cue rapid flu-like symptoms, hospitalization, death.

Rumours were already trending—this was during the internet's heyday—but she was the first one where they linked the disease to a dog, one of the last where they referred to it as a flu.

Before this, I sometimes fed leftover tacos to the skinny Weimaraner who slinked around our truck. No more. One night, she pelted from the shadows and ripped my shoulder – she literally leaped through the air. The other guys pulled her off and went at her with a frying pan. I just lay on the ground and covered my face with my arm thinking, oh fuck, my life is over.

They got me a taxi, water and a new shirt, paid the driver. No one said goodbye.

Back home I tasted the carpeting and tried to pass out. Not sure how sick I was. I felt dazed, anticipatory even, stuck in that pause between lightning and thunder. Hours poured by like this, dark to light to dark.

My mother eventually called, saying to stay in, ration the food I had. She didn't mention Dad, so I didn't ask. I thought she would've sounded different if he wasn't still alive. I got up and ate.

By then the bite on my back was a crusted purple rift, looked like any puncture wound. Not even infected—I was scared to touch it for the first few days, then got over myself; slathering antiseptic cream. The scab melted like gelatine.

I lost a lot of my mass during those weeks. When I finally left the apartment for good I was skinny and I'd grown a sparse beard I couldn't stop feeling. Everyone was travelling light.

A few months later, exiting a leafy trail, I finally recognized someone. This guy, I didn't really know in college—and we just dropped to the ground and cried. It was after that I tried to quit being so alone.

Stabbed

Joy Manné

And so I heard my mother saying to him, in an unusual voice for her: not sassy, not scratchy, not snivelly—a straight kind of voice, 'You lied, Mick. You said you were clean but we have AIDS, the baby and me—,' and through a crack in the kitchen door where I spy on them, I saw her seize the ceramic carving knife and stab at him; but Mick is beery, big and strong, and I wasn't going to wait for the worst when he grasped her wrist and would have gotten hold of the knife—I leaped into the room like a long-jump champion, gripped the knife in both hands and gouged it up into his gut, and then we breathed out, my mother and I, and although I'm only twelve, I'm big for my age, and we sat down together and planned what to do, woman to woman, like we did when Mom stabbed Dad.

Into My Own Parade

Robert Lopez

There were people everywhere, like it was a parade. In fact, I think it was a parade. Some of the people in the parade were drinking, others laughing and singing. I think it may've been a holiday, something worthy of celebration.

I was out for a walk but I had no real destination.

What makes this a story is I was about to be married. My bride's name was Constantly and she was supposed to wait for me with the officiate. I told them I had to go check on something, that I'd be right back. I told them to wait here.

She said thank you but I'm ambulatory now.

She was right. A year ago, when I met her, she was bed-ridden. She'd been in bed her whole life. The sores were the worst part, she said.

Now she walks everywhere, to the stores, to the markets, up hills, down aisles.

It's something like a miracle and everyone knows it.

This is when I asked her to marry me again, but another time, when it's more convenient for everyone, when everyone has had a chance to calm down. I said this as I was walking. She was right behind me the whole time.

I told her I wanted to have her children and raise them to be responsible citizens who held down jobs and paid taxes, but not right now. I needed more time. What I wanted more than anything was to be domesticated.

She asked me to come with her to the Irish pub across the street so she could make a counter-offer.

I considered going, but got waylaid by the people marching in garish costumes. I had no choice but to fade into my own parade and that's how I ended up.

She couldn't be stopped, though. She kept on walking like it was nothing, like she'd been doing it forever. She never once turned around, looked back. I watched her go and was proud.

Everyone in the parade cheered her on.

The Thieves are Coming. They are Taking It All.

Mary Lynn Reed

The last time I kissed you, it was about to rain. I stood on the street and held an umbrella by my side. When you drove away, I watched the light turn red. I felt the sharp wind.

I'm giving an exam and I'm running late and the copy machine is broken and I'm darting from room to room but the staff is gone and there's no chalk to write on the board and the problems are long and time is ticking away and I stand at the front of the hall, mouth agape, and then the bell rings.

On Sunday nights, I iron. With mist and steam and a firm hand.

I walk through the mall, carrying my cat on my shoulder. He's scared of the noise and lights and movement, but he stays there, claws digging into my skin.

When I was ten, I had a horse named Pride. He wasn't fully broken, and threw me off every chance he got. Dad held the reins while I went inside to wash blood off my face. He told me to get back on, and I did.

An entire crew of thieves slip through the cracks in my wooden house. They are taking everything I own. Plates out of cabinets, books off shelves, sofas, TVs, microwave oven. No time elapses between full house and empty. Everything is gone. I peek through the window, trying to remember what had been there.

On my boy's 20th birthday, I stopped at Party City and bought a fuzzy tiara. I took a video of him playing like a kitten again. His joy lasted a few seconds. Then he curled back into his spot next to my pillow. Three weeks later, the vet swaddled him in a deep brown towel. When his head fell gently against my arm, I prayed he was dreaming, soft and sweet.

You arrive at my doorstep with nothing but the clothes you are wearing and dark creases in your brow. It's my house but my parents are living upstairs. Dad is taking a nap and Mom is cooking. I lead you to my room, as if we're kids. But we know the truth. That you are 65 and I am 51 and this is finally it. The waiting is over. Your blue jeans are worn through at the knees.

Not a Horror Story

Jonathan Taylor

She was disappointed in the house. No blood dripped from the walls. The doors didn't shut by themselves. There were no bangs, murmurings and cries during the night. That bothered her more than anything: the quiet, the stillness. When her husband was away and the bed was empty, there wasn't even any breathing.

A house like this, where such horrors had taken place – where, according to the local paper, a neglected child had been cut up and left to die – shouldn't be quiet. She knew that from *The Shining*: the house should *remember* – it should remember why they'd got it so cheap, in an otherwise-desirable North London cul-de-sac. The horrors that had happened within these walls – though they weren't extreme enough to have caused the house to be bulldozed – should have left traces, ghosts, scratching in the walls, strange flowers flourishing in the garden. Instead, it was all too neat, carpeted, magnolia.

She decided to make up for the house's lack in this respect by painting the front room scarlet. Ignoring her husband's half -hearted criticisms, she purposely left drips drying in the paint, to look like blood.

Next, she drilled a large hole in the ceiling above the landing, all the way up to the attic, in order to create the kind of cold spot she had seen in any number of horror movies.

At night, when her husband was away, she'd leave the radio on downstairs – quiet, detuned – so disembodied voices, fuzz, pops and screeches reached her in bed.

She bought a doll which intermittently gurgled and cried,

and buried it underneath one of the loose floor-boards in the front room. As the batteries in the doll gradually wore out, the noises deepened to baritone, distorted into growls. Her husband didn't notice, didn't seem to hear it, when back home from his business trips to Bangkok, or wherever it was he went.

And none of it – not the paint, the hole in the ceiling, the radio, the buried doll – had any more effect on her than it did on her husband: she didn't feel the cold in the cold spot; the hairs on the back of her neck stubbornly refused to stand on end; her body refused to tremble or shiver in the dark; and her dreams remained undisturbed, suburban, magnolia.

She felt nothing.

So finally, one night when her husband was away again, she wandered downstairs into the kitchen, took out one of the steak knives, and made cuts in her arms and legs, not unlike those she had seen in the newspaper photos of the dead child.

At least the cuts hurt.

Stepping Out

Jenny Woodhouse

Friday is her birthday. Thirty-five, half her life. Lunch with the girls. Sole in a cream sauce, tiramisu. Full of food, she checks the fitness monitor on her wrist, her present to herself, because it's time to take care of herself. She's only done fifteen hundred steps, so she walks home.

On Saturday she goes shopping. Eight thousand. She buys a dress, size twelve. It will soon fit.

Sunday: the big push. They go for a country walk. Her wrist clocks up twelve thousand and she is high with success. The scales don't see any change.

On Monday she gets up early and walks instead of taking the bus. Ten thousand.

So on Tuesday she walks home as well. She manages twelve thousand. She finds him grumpy. He was woken too early, and now he's waiting for his supper. She rewards him with a rich bolognese. She tries the new dress. The zip jams.

Twelve thousand again on Wednesday, disappointing. She strides back and forth in front of Coronation Street till he shouts at her to stop.

On Thursday she arrives early at the office. Time for a few more steps. She walks on: five hundred, two thousand. It's easy to rack them up. She keeps going and she's fifteen minutes late starting work.

'Better be on time tomorrow!' says her boss. She doesn't hear.

On Friday she's determined to beat Thursday's fifteen thousand. She strides past the office and carries on, all day.

Thirty thousand. Her feet ache, her legs can hardly carry her, her waist feels trimmer. She is elated, but the scales don't agree. Nor does her boss, in an angry email.

All night she walks in her dreams.

'It's doing me good!' she tells him on Saturday morning. She eats her buttery toast walking round and round the kitchen. And she carries on, out of the front door, across the town and out the other side, and beyond.

Gabriel

Steven Moss

I first met Gabriel in the security lodge. An affable French Algerian, always smiling. One of the jobs he had was searching our bags as we left. Gabriel or Gabe as I took to calling him, was a nice guy. We started there about the same time, and he didn't speak a lot of English, so I spent a little time chatting to him at the end of my shift, teaching him phrases and such. It got so we started a competition to see who could learn the best insults in each other's language, though the more complicated ones he taught me only stayed in my head as long as it took me to get to my car each night.

As the weeks dragged into months, the job began to batter me down. The starts got earlier, the finishes later, my eyes itched from the chemicals we made.

'My friend,' Gabe said, watching me slump away one night. 'You look like the job is, how you say, *doing you in the ass.*' He laughed.

All I could offer was a tired *'Putain de merde,'* in reply.

By the second year Gabe chatted fluently with the students we employed on summer placements. I hurried through the lodge, arriving with a brief *'Ca va? Tres bien, tres bien,'* I didn't have the energy to teach or learn any more insults, I was slowly falling apart. Late night takeouts and cheap wine after shift just to get me to sleep were taking their toll in weight gain and giving me a teenager's complexion. I swapped notes with my wife, she left me messages every now and then reminding me about appointments for the kids and plays I'd missed at their school.

One uncomfortably warm night, I'd finished late as usual and Gabe was on shift. 'Hey,' he said. *'Ca va?'* He appraised me, like a dog crawling in the heat and began taking an idle look through my bag. 'You look knacker*ed*,' he said, his accent still heavy on the end of each word. He stopped his search and placed his hand on my shoulder. 'My friend this is not good.' He pulled me to him, his rough cheek on mine. 'Do you ever think,' he whispered 'we are passing through, Dant*e's* Hell? Huh? Sene*ca* said, treat each day as a separate life. Each day— is a *new* day, huh?'

I thought about my wife, the kids I didn't see, about jacking the job and doing something else with my life and then he laughed, a big throaty roar. 'Ha! This is all *bull crap*, yes? I got it from the students. They are all...' and he whirled a finger round his temple for effect, '...craz*y*.' He laughed and pushed my belongings back into place and turned to me, smiling.

'Until tomorrow,' he said, and almost as an afterthought, pulled the zip tight on my bag.

Bliss Street

Peter Wortsman

Directly opposite me on the Number 7 train sits your prototypical New Yorker in a narrow brimmed, non-descript, gray felt hat and a London Fog gray trench coat huddling behind a newspaper. Could be my late father, himself a master at folding his *Times* with crisp pleats into ever narrower vertical wedges to fit the shrinking elbow room at rush hour. Thus immersed and anesthetized into a soothing numbness by the tabloid tragedies of his fellow man, the New Yorker preserves an illusion of privacy by never looking his fellow human in the eye.

Whenever I pass a certain subway stop, though my dad's been dead and gone for almost three decades, I still scan the platform, half-expecting to spot him leaning against a pillar folding his *Times*. Every platform harbours its resident ghosts.

This particular nocturnal commuter makes no pretence of scanning the day's news. It's too late for such a charade, the 9-to-5'ers being long since planted before their TV screens feeding on the evening news. My man, as I only now notice, is gripping the paper upside-down in his trembling white knuckles.

But why?

Presently, as the train screeches round a hairpin curve, his hat tilts first into, then out of the turn, the blocked felt hesitating for a fleeting instant, till finally, no longer able to resist centrifugal temptation, it tumbles into the mess of renegade objects on the floor: lost buttons, cans and bottles.

Dropped accidentally or deliberately discarded, this lawless collection is free to indulge the wild delinquent desire to roll. No New Yorker in his right mind would reach his hand out to retrieve a fallen object, however precious, from the vicious snouts of that savage horde. The subway floor is off-limits, a precinct of virtual infection not even the clean-up crews dare sweep. Oblivious to prudence and propriety—I must have been out of my mind—I reach for the hat, and not a moment too soon, for a gang of broken bottles is already hurtling my way.

"Your hat, sir!" I cry out above the screech and clatter.

"Thanks!" comes the muffled reply, more echo than row.

And then, like a secret grown sick of itself, the newspaper falls, revealing the absence of a face. No nose, no eyes. Holes instead. Flaps of skin where eyes ought to hang, and in the middle, a horizontal slit twisting upwards into a grinning crescent as he leaps up and scurries out at Bliss Street.

Never Going to Fall for Modern Love

Sharon Telfer

She counts his heartbeats, knows each step he takes. Better than yesterday, not as good as last week. His red line tracks the grid, leading her up one street, sharp turn down the avenue, spiking like a market in meltdown.

They make sure to share meals – his eggs over easy, her cheese and pickle sandwich. The brightness of the food startles them, makes each greedy for the other's unfiltered colours.

She is glazing over at a PowerPoint when his words buzz across her heart, sharp as a tattooist's needle. In the comfort break, she slips into a cubicle, thumbs up the message. His image streaks past, leaving her breathless. Face to the dryer, she blasts away her longing. Raises her eyebrows at a colleague, 'Meeting culture!', as they lean into the mirror, putting their faces to rights.

Later, she pours a glass of red, rustles up pasta with broccoli and anchovies while they chat. Enough for two. She'll pack the rest cold for the office tomorrow. "Dangerous 'hood," he crackles, flips so she can see the park squirrels sussing out a move on his bagel.

When he goes back to work, she takes a drive past his block. Each time she has the dumb idea she might catch some glimpse of him, his hand pulling the front door to, his coattail flicking round the corner. The view never changes: the same parked cars under the same leafless trees, the pixelated stranger turning to stare.

Running her bath, she reads the menu from his local bar, chooses what he might buy her: salt beef and pickles, maybe, clam chowder.

When he comes home, she watches him shower, losing him in the steam, his singing ragged under the pounding water. As he dries, she carefully undresses for him. Behind her stands the wardrobe where his shirts – the ones that didn't make the cut – hang limp. He stretches back on the bed she has never slept in. On his bedside table he keeps that photo of the beach, the wind tangling their hair together, someone's red kite hovering above them like a blessing. Some nights, she sees it's missing. Has he shoved it in a drawer, flattened it in haste, forgetting to turn it face-side up after some unseen late-night visitor has gone?

Their chat dwindles to a murmur, then a sigh. Their hands scroll down their silvered bodies, fingers pinch, drag and swipe. Afterwards, he tells her he loves her, waits for her to turn out the lamp before cutting the connection.

She pictures him then, standing, dressing, his evening just beginning. She tries to resist playing tag, searching for him at parties she hasn't been invited to given by people she has never met.

They say it's the blue light that stops you sleeping. Messes with the melatonin, like jet lag. That must be why she lies in the dark, open-eyed, wrapped in his frayed T-shirt, trying to remember the taste of his lips.

Unseen

Marie Gethins

The year I learned the word *welt*, my best friend taught me the meaning of *half-truth*, although neither of us knew the term at the time.

In those days good parents smacked their children. Boisterous public behaviour earned a clatter across the back of your head, with observers nodding approval. At home, my parents kept a wooden paddle for more severe punishment. It resided in a kitchen drawer, just under the knives. As an adult I asked them why they chose this implement. They said it didn't leave a mark.

My best friend's father preferred a belt. On Saturday mornings she and I took swimming lessons together. My friend changed in a toilet stall, often wearing a top over her swimsuit. One morning I heard her whisper a curse. Through the thin, white door I asked what was wrong. She'd forgotten a t-shirt. I loaned her one of mine. When she let me into the stall, I saw a scattering of long red marks between her shoulder blades. "Welts—from my dad's belt buckle," she said.

After that we shared the stall, giggling our contorted limbs into bright lycra each week, a rectangular world for two. Before the final lesson, my friend's back had three white domes encircled in red. She caught my stare and shrugged. "He's using something different, that's all."

Later outside the sports centre, we walked to where my mother and my friend's father chatted. They leaned against cars, absorbed the sun's heat. He smiled and took a drag on his cigarette. The paper disappeared into grey ash, end glowing orange. My stomach shifted. Her father tossed the butt onto the hot tarmac, his toe crushed it flat. He said good-bye. My friend shuffled in his wake, head bowed, hair dripping. I watched her droplet trail evaporate.

The Girl in Purple

Bobbie Ann Mason

Near dawn, Dennis Moore saw the iron gate to the courtyard inch open and the wisp of a girl squeeze through, clanging the gate behind her. Two minutes later, on the boardwalk, she halted as if for an invisible dog, then resumed her dog-walker gait. He followed her down this wooden walkway, known as the Promenade. The surf, retreating as if pushed by the hurrying sun, murmured and slurped. The girl, he could see now, was dressed in purple, and she wore a thick long scarf twisted in an elaborate slip-knot around her throat.

His thoughts wandered. The Auguste Macke poster of "Promenade 1913" above his mantel. Andy Kaufman wrestling women in the videos he had watched. Lisbeth Salander with the dragon tattoo. The nutrition facts on the back of the granola bar in his pocket.

The girl in purple was coughing. She paused on the Promenade and coughed repeatedly. Something had gone down the wrong way. He knew the feeling.

This was the right moment to grab her, but he felt dizzy and sluggish. He had to concentrate. She was lighting a cigarette, cupping it from the beach breeze. He saw that her scarf was a tartan. He thought of Scotch tape. Quietly, he tiptoed behind her along the bare boards. When Mark Twain steered the riverboat around the bend where the Mississippi meets the Ohio, he had to proceed very carefully. But he dumped Huck and Jim there on a flimsy raft in those dangerous waters where Illinois, Missouri, and Kentucky come together to shake hands. Now Dennis Moore had to go very carefully, pitty-pat. He could not stop himself now. This time he would do it.

A light bulb lit in his head. *Fuck hen.* Until this moment the spoonerism of Huck Finn had never occurred to him. That old jokester, Twain, was probably still laughing, wherever he was. The granola bar would taste good right now. Pay attention! She coughed again. The scarf was many shades of purple, flashing in the sudden sunrise.

Originally published by New Flash Fiction:
http://newflashfiction.com/bobbie-ann-mason/

The Great Forgotten Language

Conor Houghton

My boss Paul said that since it was Patrick's Day I should bring them all to an Irish pub. He kept insisting. "It will be craic" he said and laughed, pleased with himself. I wanted to hit him; instead I thought of his girlfriend Sarah naked and sitting tailor style on my bed, rubbing the bottom of her big toe with her thumb and squinting against the Sunday-morning light. Then I remembered later, her leaving and me not saying anything that meant anything as she paused by the door. Out of badness, I decided to bring them to Kavanaghs.

It was only eight when we arrived but there was a group of lads close to fighting in the back. I sat us all down under a framed photo of the Free Derry mural and Paul came with me to get drinks. Fiddling with his cash as usual he dropped a fiver and a big lump of a man at the bar put his foot over it and stared Paul down. I pretended not to notice, not sure which side I was on. When Paul left with the first of the pints, the barman said to me "right shower you have with you". "Paddy's Day, you know yourself," I replied, my accent coming back without me willing it.

I looked around. An old guy had one hand in through the fly of his filthy trousers; a drunk with a baby in a pushchair kept falling off his stool. Someone called over to the barman asking would Gráinne sing a song for the day that was in it. Like a magic trick, the barman bent down and lifted a girl of about nine up from where she'd been sitting, probably she'd been on a small stool reading the Beano she still had in one hand. He set her on the counter top and after pretending to be shy she began to sing 'Raglan Road'.

Some bent their heads, some parted their lips, all were silent to better feel the beauty of it. That grim bar became like a church with the wonder of her voice. We thought of home, of when we were happy. In my head I was ten and in the yard, holding the piebald cob for the blacksmith who was singing 'Raglan Road' softly to himself as he worked at a hoof. A great shaft of light coming down from a gap in the clouds showed God was in Heaven. The cob was restless and I kept saying "come on, settle down" and the blacksmith told me not to say "come on" if I wanted to horse to stay still, he told me that sometimes you had to use words that only mean one thing.

The song ended and we all struggled to hear it still in the noise from the street outside. When that didn't work anymore I left Kavanaghs and caught a taxi to Sarah's building and finally said words to her that only mean one thing.

It All Ends

Rupert Dastur

'You voted for him?' I say, unable to hide my disbelief.

'You don't understand,' says Billy. 'It's time we took a stand.'

'Against what? Decency?'

'Islam,' says Billy.

'Jesus,' I say.

'Didn't throw people off buildings,' says Billy.

I stop because we both know he is smarter than this.

We sit on the veranda, sipping coffee, watching families pass by beneath us laden with weekend groceries. I wonder what assumptions they'd make if they cared to look up. Billy is tall and thin; the hair on one side of his head is cut shorter than the other. He pulls on the cigarette.

'But his vice—'

'Is a fucking liability,' agrees Billy. 'Another fag?' he pushes the packet towards me.

'I never say no,' I say.

'Amen to that,' says Billy. He gives the tightest of smiles and then leans right forward so that his head is nearly on my lap. 'You weren't *there*,' he says.

I have no response.

Orlando. For us, the name has not lost its horror. And yet I want to say something. Anything.

I use the word *home-grown* and Billy gives me the same look he had when I told him things weren't ever going to work out between us.

'Home-grown?' he says. 'You would think we were talking about fucking house plants.'

I stand to go.

'Stay,' he says. 'Please.'

There is nothing harder in this world than saying no to the person you love. And I do not have the strength, not today, even though much of what we once were has passed. I sit and let the sun warm the back of my neck.

'How is Dominic?' he asks.

'Well,' I say. 'Working hard.'

'Thank you for coming today,' says Billy. 'I've been meaning to tell you something.' His sudden prosaic formality has me on edge.

What he says fulfils the purpose of my breakfast invitation with devastating simplicity. He does not start crying – he was never a weeper – but his eyes turn red, as if they are forming their own cages of despair.

'I always thought I'd grow into one of those pervy old queens,' says Billy. 'People keep telling me I've got to be *positive*... as if I haven't heard enough of the fucking word.' He grins. It is a terrible thing to see, the smile of a condemned man.

I tell him about drugs he already knows, health programmes, new research. I sound like an advice leaflet that haunts clinic desks, complete with stock images of sick patients giving hopeful thumbs-up.

And then: 'Is that why you voted for him?'

'You don't change, do you James?' replies Billy, shaking his head. 'It all ends. All of it. So what does it matter?'

'*That's* your answer? What about the rest of us, Billy?' I say.

'You see,' he says, watching me rise, 'it all fucking ends.'

A Thousand Years

Tim Stevenson

Edmund could imagine it, thousands of Danes rushing down the hill through the mud to meet the English in a last desperate battle, the English King on horseback shouting hopelessly as he was overpowered, his men falling beneath Scandinavian steel.

He pictured the King, stripped of his armour and his jewellery, paraded in his hessian leggings in front of the laughing troops.

That was why he was here, wandering up and down in the endless mud, swinging his metal detector for thousand-year-old treasures.

He was hating every minute.

Jen didn't like it much either, not that she ever came with him. She stood, arms crossed on the doorstep, as he loaded the car, and scowled at him as he drove away.

The detector whined as he kicked open another clod of earth to reveal the spring from a clothes peg, another reminder of a job he wasn't doing, another responsibility shirked.

The machine at his feet whined, beeped once, fell sideways.

Then it shrieked.

The noise pierced the drizzle and scattered the birds.

It was a three-a.m. car alarm of noise, a supermarket screaming baby, a fan-belt howl of a sound.

Edmund began to dig. His hands tore at the earth. Grass and roots breaking as he ripped and burrowed, the sodden loam yielding until something glittered in the muck. Something small, and yellow, and heavy.

Edmund rubbed it between his fingers.

A ring. Old gold.

It rattled in his pocket all the way home, weighed heavy in his hand as he pushed in into the darkness between the rhododendrons, and, as if knowing the story it was part of, allowed itself to be buried.

Edmund waited.

Jen was in the kitchen.

"Come outside," he said.

"Why?" Her arms were crossed, tighter than before.

"Have a go with the detector. It'll be fun," he said.

Jen looked at the grey sky, the hopeless man standing on the lawn.

"Oh, do fuck off," she said.

She moved out on Wednesday, the single suitcase rattling behind her like the dog they'd never bought.

And that was it, six months, over.

Rather than contemplate the washing up, he joined a club. Serious men talked about coil diameters and waterproof headphone connectors, while Edmund nodded and listened instead to the other people lined up along the bar, and their laughter.

One day, after what would seem like a thousand years, someone might laugh with him like that, the right kind of laugh, an echo of his own to let him know there was something to find, something to dig up, something underneath.

He would drive them home and guide their shaking hands down towards the earth between the rhododendrons, and there would be a different kind of high-pitched squeal, not the detector lying in the dirt, not laughter far away at the other end of the bar.

It would be delight.

Friends

Miranda Kate

She'd switch on the music and one by one they'd arrive.

They hung out with her daily, enjoying the same music, talking about the same things, just enjoying good company. Every morning after her husband had gone to work she would wonder who would come.

When she had first moved here, she'd struggled. When you are born a city girl, village life was hard to get used to, even if you weren't in a foreign country. He'd spent two years convincing her it was the place to be: all his family were there, his friends, it would be a great community to be in. But she hadn't been prepared for the culture difference, or the language barrier. They all could speak English, couldn't they? It didn't occur to her that they might not want to.

Her favourites would always turn up, some making an entrance. They'd talk about life, love, how they all knew each other. She'd even get up and dance, sometimes sing. Kate would always get up with her and they'd make quite a show. She'd laugh with them, even flirt with them. She'd feel alive, real—visible. She had found the place and the people she belonged to.

But she'd watch the clock, be ready for when her husband came home. The house would be tidy, dinner prepared. He didn't know about them. It wasn't important.

She'd tried to integrate with her husband's friends, but it was difficult. They never spoke slowly enough or simplified the language; no translation, no effort to bring her into the discussion, just chatting amongst themselves, not caring if she was there or not. But they'd made it clear from the beginning she wasn't welcome.

They'd held a welcome back party, but one she wasn't invited to—because they weren't going to wait for her to arrive. why would they? He was the long-lost friend returning to their folds, not her. He'd returned without her to get everything ready and they'd surprised him with it. He'd called her late that night to tell her about it: the big dinner, the drinking, presenting him with a crown & cape—all thirty of them. He'd had no idea then how much it'd upset her.

But she had steeled herself and joined him, finding him there at the airport with a single red rose and a balloon, keen to have her with him. And she'd waited for his friends to come and say welcome, but no one did.

And now, years on, she'd gotten used to it: the not hearing from any of them, not seeing them, even though they lived a stones throw from her house. It didn't matter anymore; she had her own friends to hang out with who were there for her every day. They'd always want her company, be interested in her conversation, make her feel special, important – an insider. After all she'd created them in her head, and thank goodness, otherwise she'd be truly lonely.

Bunnahabhain

Nuala Ní Chonchúir

Jenny wears a clap-and-shriek outfit to court. But that's Jenny, the gaudier the better, and this dress is sunflowers on mulch, paired with nasty grey shoes. I know she's saying, 'Take me as you see me, this is me, there is no other'. But, for the trial, I'd hoped for the alternate version of my mother, the one who sometimes opts for muted, the one who can tone it all down. We stand in the hallway of the courthouse, waiting to be called, and Jenny seems calm despite everything.

She stayed in my house last night and we drank whiskey: Auchentoshan, Kilbeggan, Talisker, Lagavulin and more, all the bottles lined up on my kitchen table. We didn't talk about court or the teenage girl she ploughed down with her car – and crippled – while drunk. Jenny preferred, as always, to focus her mind elsewhere. Outwards, backwards.

'All I ever wanted from him was a house with a garden,' she said. My father had finally left her, alone in their flat, after this latest bout of chaos. 'I wanted a garden rimmed with trees. Trees linked and dancing in an endless ring-a-rosy.'

I snorted. 'You wanted trees like children but not *actual* children.'

'Exactly,' Jenny said, sipping from her glass and staring at me. 'But you're all right, aren't you?' She waved her hand at my kitchen, as if having a house meant my life must be good and sound and proper.

'Unh,' I said.

She read out the labels on the whiskey bottles. 'Balvenie, Bunnahabhain, Glenkinchie.' She drank. 'Bunnahabhain: bottom of the river. That's probably where I should be.'

'Your old refrain,' I said. As a child, when I irritated Jenny, she threatened to throw herself into the Liffey and float away. *See how you'd like it then!* 'I lost weeks of sleep when you'd say that to me. I'd sicken myself imagining you stuck in riverweed, gone from me forever.' My mother, a dark Ophelia, rotting in dank water.

She didn't respond but her face shifted and she had the decency to look a small bit contrite. I poured her a glass of Bunnahabhain and together we let its nutty, oaky burn heat our throats and bellies.

'Are the parents here?' Jenny says, and her face is untamed, frightened. I've never seen fear on my mother before and it alters her.

'I'm sure they are,' I say.

'Do they hate me? Does the girl?'

I put my hand on her floral sleeve and feel the *tremens* there. I want to say, 'It's enough that you hate yourself,' but I can't.

'You'll be okay, Jenny,' I say.

She leans into me and I take her into the crook of my arm; she is small and ridiculous and sad in her Van Goghian dress. I look out the door of the courthouse, at the Liffey's pea-soupy meander to the bay, and I hope that we will all be okay.

Let Them Know Me By My Teeth

Michael Loveday

The odour of garlic drifted from the kitchen as waiters in blue shirts hustled by. I was sitting in a corner, running my finger around the edge of a cardboard coaster – an advert for WinBingo.com. It was a delaying tactic: I didn't want to face what had happened. I waited for a Greek salad and an even more self-denying sparkling water. This week, more luxury than that seemed out of place.

Two teenage girls were smirking at a neighbouring table. I thought they might be giggling at me. I caught a phrase – *granddad* something – but told myself it didn't fit and re-opened my diary at the first empty page. I watched my pen scuttle over the paper. It was like talking to someone, talking to no one; a hopeless attempt at remedy.

I spun through the hamster-wheel of disappointments – first the news from my lawyer, next the clumsy embrace of the welfare state, then my wife moving me out and blocking my calls. I hadn't even been offered time to pack: only an hour's notice and a threat to call the police. Yet the letdowns were oddly familiar, like being trapped in conversation with an old friend.

"You look busy," said the waitress, gleaming at me with a North American smile. I waited a beat. "I'm a writer," I lied. I couldn't stop my left hand from pulling the diary an inch closer towards me.

"What are you…?" she asked, looking at my upside-down words, then faltering into silence and looking elsewhere. She turned back, and her gaze settled on the WinBingo coaster.

"Had any luck?" I glowered back at her. "No. I guess if you had," she added, "you wouldn't be here."

A pause. "Do you want anything else?" Fucking peace and quiet, I answered, silently. And then, as if in sarcastic response, the fire alarm sounded. "Excuse me," she said. She scurried over to her station.

All the customers sat listening, looking at each other. No one seemed to know what to do. A collective conspiracy emerged: wait for instructions. People picked up their knives and forks again; bursts of embarrassed laughter carried around the room.

Then came the manager over the tannoy: *Please proceed to the exit. Do not stop to collect your belongings. There is no cause for alarm.* Slowly, reluctantly, customers abandoned their meals and filed out of the restaurant.

I wasn't going anywhere. I felt sure that some insight would surface eventually; but with each word I wrote, my old life extended further and further out of reach, like an apple dangling above a young man's hand. Everyone else was falling into line with the manager's voice calling out over the sound system like a petty god. What did it matter if they found only my charred and shrivelled remains? Let them know me by my teeth! I kept filling the journal, top to bottom, page after page, while the siren shrilled. The apple was there, somewhere. I was going to grab it.

Horsewhip

Lex Williford

Last summer, while my brother Nate and I were cleaning out our parents' cluttered Dallas garage, I pulled from a liquor box the horsewhip our grandmother Eveline had punished my father and his brother R. E. with after their father'd died— cracked leather and frayed tassels bound in tight knots. The same ratty horsewhip Eveline's Great Aunt Bama'd used to whip her with after her father abandoned her at the post office in Iuka, Mississippi, and never came back. The same horsewhip, our father swore, that her grandfather'd used on the bare backs of slaves he'd lost after the Civil War.

When our white-haired father limped into the garage moments later, I asked him, "Did your mother really hit you with this thing?" and he said, "You're goddamn right she did. And it was the best goddamn thing that ever happened to me."

I glanced at Nate and watched the straight line of his lips press together white, the muscles fisting at his jaws, and when he glanced back at me, I must've been wearing the same expression, as if the answer to the question we'd both been asking ourselves all our lives had finally shown itself like the moment our father was born, not a foetus's soft skull and fontanelle crowning beneath his mother's mons, not his slicked head sliding into the cupped palms of the inept midwife, but instead his shrivelled and puckered red ass, sticking out and stuck there, the breech birth that almost killed our father and his mother both.

A Terrier's Limits

Sophie Rosenblum

Claw marks line my calves where my dog has been fucking me. I'm sure if they were thicker, sturdier, cows instead of calves, we'd both be having a better time. Instead, we lie on a patch-wool blanket in a field, blood trickling down my leg.

In an effort to create pillow talk, she laps at the streams that leak from the backs of my recently punctured knees. Her tongue is thick, rough, and she looks up at me with a face of such slant-eyed contentment that I can almost see the greater good.

When she's had her fill, I hook her leash and she leads me back to the car. We pass chickens with hairdos like showgirls, plumes of white feathers atop their scrawny, screaming heads. The leather lead grows taught between us as a new temptation picks out space between her ears.

Originally published in Flash Forward, Volume III, 2010.

Communication

Mark Connors

Blink once for yes and twice for no. Alternatively, you could just start fucking talking to me again.

Free Hugs

Gary Duncan

The man in the beige turtleneck is offering free hugs, no strings attached.

"Come and get 'em," he says, arms outstretched. "Get 'em before they're gone."

He's been here an hour, outside Starbucks, and still no takers.

He thinks the split nose and the fat lip might be a problem. Knows you can't be hugging people looking like that, all smashed up. Puts people on edge, sends off the wrong signals.

There's no sign of the kid who thumped him yesterday, the kid with the bony fists, but the man in the beige turtleneck doesn't hold a grudge.

"A good hug," he'd said to the policeman. "That's all he needs."

He'd dabbed his still-bleeding lip and sniffled. "It does sadden me though. The lack of empathy. The lack of *compassion*. You know?"

The policeman had nodded sympathetically. The man in the beige turtleneck stepped forward, arms wide. "Come on, officer, I think we both need a big one."

*

The couple at the window table are on their first date. They watch the man in the beige turtleneck with the beat-up face. The passersby swerving out of his way. They're both divorced, both too old to be doing this kind of thing, both wishing they'd stayed at home.

The woman, whose name is Hellen — Hellen with a double "l" — has ordered a latte but hasn't touched it. She needs to pee — she *really* needs to pee — but doesn't want to get up and make the long, lonely walk to the toilet at the far end of the café.

The man, Peter, wonders if he'll ever get to know this woman well enough — if he'll ever get to know *any* woman well enough — to explain why his wife left him.

He finishes his espresso — his second — and watches as the woman whose name he has temporarily forgotten crosses her legs and looks anxiously over his shoulder.

He tells her about the man in the beige turtleneck.

"I saw everything," he says. "The kid punching him, punching him in the face, over and over."

He says he talked to the policeman, described the kid to him. The kid, the assailant. Says the policeman wrote it all down on a spiral notepad with a stubby pencil but misspelled the word assailant: one "s" instead of two. Peter says he let it pass. Didn't think it was that important, considering.

*

Peter thinks this isn't going very well. Hellen — he remembers her name now — hasn't said much and still hasn't touched her coffee. He senses she doesn't like him. Something in the angle of her mouth. Maybe they should have gone for a walk instead, or arranged to meet at one of the group's social events. Safety in numbers. Bingo. Bowling. Something like that.

He gets up and walks over to the counter to order another espresso.

The man in the beige turtleneck is hugging an old woman, his arms clamped around her like he's never going to let her go.

The Sun on the Dash

Stephen Tuffin

They were parked in Northdown Park, a fact Patrick had made a joke about earlier. Mac had grinned but hadn't fully understood. On the doors of the lorry, written in bold letters, were the words:

McCaulley and MacCulloch Ltd
Civil Engineering and Ground Works.
Established 1958

Inside the cab Patrick McCaulley and Charlie MacCulloch were having lunch.

'Ham for you,' Patrick said handing a slab of sandwich to Mac. 'Cheese for me.'

They ate; their hands dirty from the trench they'd been digging.

'How deep we got to go?' Mac said through a mouthful of sandwich.

'Three feet.'

'How deep is it now?'

'A gnat's cock shy of two feet.'

They didn't speak again until the sandwiches were all gone.

*

Patrick rummaged inside his khaki tucker bag until he found a banana and a couple of satsumas.

'You want the banana, I suppose,' he said handing it to Mac.

Mac peeled and devoured the banana in two great gobfulls.

Patrick stripped a satsuma, dropping the peel expertly into the foot-well beside him.

The dashboard was home to Mac's collection of red tops, plus a pair and a half of gloves and an old balaclava that doubled as a rag for wiping condensation from the windscreen. Behind the driver's seat was a dog-eared map of The Isle of Thanet and a battered Manila envelope brimming with civil engineering drawings.

On the tarmac path outside, two magpies approached a piece of carrion.

'I hate magpies,' Mac sniffed.

Patrick watched the two birds for a moment, their blue-green feathers flapping angrily as they bickered over a morsel of hedgehog intestine.

'Why do you hate magpies?' Patrick said squeezing a satsuma pip between his finger and thumb, causing it to ricochet off the windscreen and into Mac's lap.

'They're fuckers,' Mac said. 'Ruthless bastards.'

'I bet you love lions though, don't you?'

'Who doesn't love lions?'

'Lions are ruthless too. And I bet you don't know why.'

'I don't.'

'Neither do they. They just are. Just like magpies.'

Mac picked at a tooth with a matchstick then examined the soggy end: 'Everybody loves lions,' he said.

'I don't,' Patrick said swallowing the last of his satsuma.

'You don't love nothing,' Mac said transferring the match from mouth to ear.

'Yes I do,' Patrick said.

'Come on then, what do you love?' Mac worked the matchstick into the dark hole of his ear.

Patrick looked longingly across the cab at his oldest and dearest friend. He studied Mac's weathered profile: the lines, the three-day stubble, the mass of matted hair. 'I...' he said, and then he fell silent.

Mac settled the soggy matchstick back into the corner of his mouth and grunted. Grabbing *The Sun* from the dashboard he tilted the open page towards Patrick. 'Would you look at the size of those beauties!' he grinned.

Dancing Partners

Diane Simmons

My classmates are in a huddle in the playground, plotting. As soon as our teacher announced the date of the Christmas party, I knew they'd start.

It's The Gay Gordons I hate the most. Last year I got in a right tangle. I'm not sure why I'm so rubbish – they've had us do Scottish country dancing since Primary One.

There's no point in me joining the plotters. I'll not get a say. Jennifer and Grace always decide everyone's partners. For weeks before the party they're off giggling, passing round notes, bagsying the gorgeous boys for themselves. Last year I got stuck with Iain MacGregor. He's not bad looking, but he's awful pale and his spikey hair makes him look like Oor Wullie.

I head off to the football field. Malcolm from my class has the ball. He always has the ball. And he's always Jennifer's dancing partner. But me and Malcolm are pals – after school most nights we're off up the playpark practising shooting goals. I bet he'd rather dance with me.

I run my fingers through my hair, try and untangle the worst of the knots and march over towards Malcolm. It's not until I'm near him that my legs begin to wobble. He smiles and kicks the ball towards me. 'Fancy a game, Isla?' he asks.

I shake my head. 'No, you're fine – I've a skirt on.'

He snorts and I look down at my skirt – it's covered in grass stains and all crumpled. 'Aye, I can see you wouldnae want to spoil it!' he says as he walks away shaking his head and laughing. I feel like that messy monkey I saw in Edinburgh zoo – the one with its fur all covered in squashed fruit.

I want to bolt, but I creep away, try not to notice him scoring another of his perfect goals. Near the playground, I spot Iain MacGregor coming towards me. He's acting awful weird – taking funny wee steps, his arms all over the place. When he starts walking backwards, then twists round, I realise he's dancing. He waves at me and runs over. 'Would you care to dance, Modom?' he asks.

He sounds stupid, but I let him take my hand.

When we've got our limbs sorted, he begins to hum the tune to the Gay Gordons and leads me through the dance. He's magnificent, in control. We get through the tricky bit no bother and he twirls me round and round like he's been practising for weeks.

When we stop and he bows, then gives me a shy wee smile, I realise he has.

Missing

Gary V. Powell

My menopausal wife, for whom a good night's sleep has become as rare as oxygen on the moon, is already awake, reading news on her iPad.

Before I've poured coffee, she informs me that Vladimir Putin's wife is missing. It's unclear if Lyudmila is "missing" missing, or merely missing from the public eye, but given her husband's reported ties to the Russian Mafia and his history as a spymaster, the fact she's missing in any sense cannot be good news for those who love Lyudmila.

Some speculate she's closeted herself because she's gained weight and chooses not to be ridiculed in the media, while other sources attribute her absence to Vlady's pursuit of former spy turned lingerie model, Anna Chapman, or resumption of his affair with Olympian, Alina Kabayeva.

Russia stretches from the Siberian tundra to the Caspian Sea. Medieval castles abound. There is plenty of space in which one might ditch an inconvenient spouse or her bloody remains.

Neither fat, nor inconvenient, my wife wonders aloud if *I* would miss *her* if *she* went missing.

I'm no spymaster. I have no gold medallist or luscious model in the wings. Short on medieval castles, I'd have to bury my wife in the crawl space if I took a hatchet to her skull. "Sure, Honey," I say. "Absolutely."

This would suffice were my wife not prone to frequent hot flashes despite the oestrogen patch worn on her belly. "Yes, but do you think *Putie* misses *Lyudy*? She's all dried up."

Our twenty-year marriage has had its challenges—the occasional falling out over finances, heated disagreements over where to live, and the suspected affairs, me with a graduate student, her with a tennis pro, but our union endures in part because I know how to respond in situations like this. "Really? Lyudmila?"

My wife stares at me over the rim of her cup, eyes hollowed out from night sweats. "But do you think Putin misses her?"

I imagine him in the cold parlours of the same residence once inhabited by Stalin. The ghosts of old Bolsheviks haunt those halls—Zinoviev, Kamenev, Trotsky, Lenin himself. On the other hand, Anna and Alina occasionally warm Vlady's bed.

I remove the coffee cup from my wife's hand and embrace her. "Sure. How could he not?"

She sags against me. "I hope so."

I'm about to pull away, when she looks up. "Don't you want to know whether *I* think *she* misses *him*?"

It shouldn't, but that one catches me by surprise. "Absolutely, I want to know. What do you think? Does Lyudmila miss Vlady?"

She stares at the birdfeeder from where our wrens have gone absent, due no doubt to the prowess of the feral cat that hunts these parts. "Maybe his physical presence," she says, "but not the rest of it."

"What do you mean, 'the rest of it'?"

She lays her hand, beneath the skin of which diminished female hormones percolate, on my hand. "You know, Sweetie, the rest of it."

Teeter, Totter, Tattle-Tale

Rachael Dunlop

My Russian dolls are balsa-thin, lushly painted in red and black, lacquered stiff. I like to keep them un-nested, lined up on my bedroom window sill, facing the world, not each other's innards. All except for the littlest one. She's a solid little pin of a thing, but roughly finished on the bottom so she topples more than she stands. Teeter, totter, tattle-tale. I have to keep her inside her next-biggest sister. Four dolls stand in a row, but I know they are five.

I sit at the kitchen table, dipping chips into the soft yolks of my fried eggs, trying not to retch and hoping Mum will ask. Just ask. I can't find a way to start the words.

The waistband of my school skirt is getting tight already, even though I'm only four months gone and eating nothing with all the nausea. I push my plate away. Mum has her back to me, staring out the kitchen window, turning a tea towel inside a cup until it squeaks. The sound of my plate sliding across the Formica gets her attention.

'All done?' she asks.

I nod and make to get up.

'Wait,' she says. 'Have a cup of tea at least.' She puts a mug in front of me, the tea barely warm, I wonder when she made it. 'Get that down you, all in one, it'll do you good.'

I'm used to my mother's reliance on tea to fix all ills. Tea is to the Irish as chicken soup is to the Jews, she always says. I wish she wouldn't. The tea is bitter. Bitter, biter, bit. I swallow it down, gagging a little at the strange aftertaste that's akin to how I imagine licking flagstones would taste.

Before I go to sleep, I touch the domed heads of each of my Russian dolls, largest to second-smallest, the curve of each pleasing under my fingers. I wonder how things will be after the baby comes. I feel like an interloper in my own life. Loping, looping, lost. I pick up the second-smallest doll and turn her top half. She's reluctant to open and the sound of the wood squeaking against itself makes me lick my fillings. With a pop she separates and the littlest doll falls into my hand. The weight of her in my palm is, I guess, more than that of all her hollow sisters put together. I put her under my pillow and go to sleep.

I wake to the taste of iron in my mouth and cramps in my belly. The blood is stamped Rorschach-like between my clamped thighs. My mother is already on the landing, the light on, waiting to usher me into the bathroom. 'Sure, didn't I tell you the tea would do you good?' she says. 'It'll all be over soon, and then it'll be back to life as we know it.'

Later, I slide my hand under my pillow to find my littlest doll. She's gone. Gone, going, ghost.

Anamnesis

Gay Degani

I remember the tick my mother tried to burn off my head with her Winston, singeing my hair, but the little sucker was stubborn so the doctor took a knife to my scalp; the time Paige walked me home from kindergarten because I'd wet my pants, her mother spotting us on the sidewalk, chasing us down, bawling me out; the excitement of getting fitted into a tiny cheerleading outfit, but never wearing it because the school principal wanted his own daughter to be the mascot; kneeling on the hard oak floor of our dining room because I'd broken a glass or sassed my dad; the day my mom was late so I walked two miles home from Girl Scouts only to have her drive up behind me, blasting her horn on Pacific Coast Highway, then hugging the air from my chest; waking to a commotion, my folks and grandmother trying to quiet my grandfather, who was roiling drunk and sticking candy in his ears; the morning we stopped by the state hospital to see him, but I had to wait in the car. It was the Deep South. August. I was sure he would die.

I don't want to forget sitting on our apartment steps on Paseo de la Playa, tightening metal skates to my saddle shoes, rolling down asphalt to the liquor store for gum or a candy bar, dime in my pocket; remembering the names of all the orchestra instruments, surprising my teacher, no less a shock to me; my fingers hovering over canasta cards trying to conjure an ace or a three to fill in my book or my run; listening to my mother's best friend from high school telling how he shot off his middle finger while hunting ducks in a sportsman's paradise; signing up for baton twirling lessons with my cousin at the park in Louisiana, picturing myself throwing the stick high into the air and catching it behind my back, but we drove home to California the next day, our car filled with smoke, heat, and silence, leaving behind Cora's jambalaya, my grandmother's gumbo, and seven watermelons icing in galvanized tubs.

I hold these memories in my mind as if I dreamt them last night, but I don't remember what day it is, where I left my phone, my tennies, the refund check from the IRS. Don't interrupt me when I'm talking because whatever I wanted to say will be instantly lost. Don't call me out of the kitchen because I'll forget to turn off the stove or the faucet or I'll leave the refrigerator door open, exhaling its chilly air. Make sure I write down our date for lunch on my calendar or I won't show up, and call me that day to remind me to *look* at the calendar because if you don't, I might head off to Target with the Sunday ads in hand, and you completely forgotten.

Sleep is a Beautiful Colour

Helen Rye

4am

5-year-old: I did a poo and it looked a bit like a snake and a bit like a man, like a sort of snake-man.

5am

5-year-old: [*Long, obscure school-based anecdote.*]

6am

5-year-old, singing: *Humpty Dumpty sat on the wall/ Wearing—* what's your favourite colour, Mummy?
Parent: Sleep.
5-year-old: Sleep's not a colour!
Parent: It's a beautiful colour.

7am

5-year-old: Heaven's a funny word. Heaven. Heaveh. Heaveh. I bet that's how chickens say it.

8am

5-year-old: I can't find the neck holes in either of these tops.
Parent: They're actually leggings.

9am

Parent *(standing barefoot in something on the upstairs landing)*: AARGGHH, AAARGGHH WHAT DID I JUST STAND IN?
5-year-old *(shifty)*: I don't know!

Parent: IS IT CAT POO?

5-year-old: It might be a plum.

Parent: What plum? From where? We don't have any plums!

5-year-old: It was in my music box. I forgot about it. It was quite furry.

10am

Parent: Come on! Hurry up! We really need to go! Are you listening to me? It's late! What are you doing?

5-year-old *(small voice)*: I was just staring at you. I can't stop looking at you, because you're so pretty.

Parent *(small voice)*: Oh.

11am

5-year-old *(eyeing supermarket shelves)*: What are those?

Parent: Brussels sprout stalks.

5-year-old: Am I allergic to them?

Parent: No. But nice try.

12pm

5-year-old, in car: I-spy-with-my-little-eye, something beginning with *L*.

Parent: Lorry? Leaf? Lamp-post…?

12.15pm

Parent: …Liability insurance? Litigation practitioner? Large Hadron Collider? Lucifer? Okay, I GIVE UP.

5-year-old: LAURA'S LITTLE BROTHER.

Parent: WHERE?

5-year-old: In the playground, yesterday. I saw him with his mum.

1pm

5-year-old *(producing paper and pen)*: Mummy, please write this: 'Dear Police, do tarantulas really exist?'

2pm

5-year-old *(in grip of enthusiasm for covering everything in blankets)*: Grandad?

Grandad: Yes?

5-year-old: You know when you get up in the morning?

Grandad: Yes?

5-year-old: And you come downstairs?

Grandad: Yes?

5-year-old: And you have your breakfast and then you sit on the sofa?

Grandad: Yes?

5-year-old: ...I'M GOING TO BURY YOU.

Grandad: …

Parent: She means a blanket fort. It's not a death threat.

3pm

Parent hoovers house ready for guest.

4pm

5-year-old *(trailing armful of freshly-uprooted weeds through house)*: Look! Whole plants! With earth and everything!

4.05pm

Parent hoovers house ready for guest.

5pm

5-year-old: I decorated the house!

Parent *(ominous feeling)*: What does that mean?

5-year-old: I cut up tinsel to make the floors pretty. And the outside steps.

5.02pm

Parent hoovers house ready for guest.

<u>5.30pm</u>
Parent hoovers outside steps, silently defying neighbours to comment.

<u>6pm</u>
Guest arrives.

<u>6.02pm</u>
5-year-old throws balloon-based craft project into air. Balloon-based craft project bursts. Balloon-based craft project, they discover, is full of flour.

<u>6.03pm</u>
Guest cleans up flour.

<u>6.03pm</u>
Parent cleans up 5-year-old.

<u>7pm</u>
5-year-old *(in bed)*: I think giants do exist.
Parent: Yeah?
5-year-old: Yes. For real. And we're just a TV programme on their tablet.
Parent: Goodnight. I love you.
5-year-old: And there's no monsters outside?
Parent *(crossing fingers behind back)*: No, my darling. There're no monsters.

The Fisher King

Christopher M Drew

Three hundred and twenty-five pictures. No. No. No.

The man has been trying for years. Every morning is the same: he showers, slips on his suit, packs his briefcase, and drives alone through the over-exposed monochrome twilight.

He hikes through the forest, unfolds a camping chair, and sits beneath the same old white willow. Sunlight blots through its wilting branches and paints the woodland in pale pastel shades of dawn.

He sets the tripod and camera, twists the lens, and attaches the remote shutter. He takes a few test shots, adjusts the settings, and waits.

He closes his eyes, just for a moment, and listens to the whisper of leaves, the lazy click of crickets, and the hypnotic adagio of the meandering stone-strewn stream. He inhales slowly, savouring the intoxicating perfume of scattered lilacs and butterfly-brushed bluebells clustered in the rain-soaked earth.

Splash. His thumb hits the shutter before his eyes snap open. He glances at the LCD. A frozen flower of water cups the tip of an iridescent blue tail. Too late.

He unscrews his flask, takes a sip of coffee. Wake up. Focus.

The bird alights on a knuckled, moss-covered branch. A minnow wriggles in its beak. It smacks the fish against the bark—w*hack, whack*—and swallows it whole.

The bird spreads its wings and flicks its tail; water droplets spray like crystal confetti through the air. It puffs its feathers, allows the breeze to scrub them dry. It turns its black dewdrop eye towards the water and waits for silver scales to flash beneath the surface.

This time, the man is ready. He is still, silent.

Blink. The bird vanishes in a blur of cyan and orange. His thumb twitches. Not yet. Not yet.

Now.

Click-click-click-click-click-click-click.

Surely, this time he has it. A fraction of a second split like an atom. The elusive, celestial convergence of speed, aperture, and light.

The perfect shot.

*

At home, after work, he uploads the pictures and scans through them. Maybe this one. No. This one? No.

No. No. No.

He prints them out, each sliver of time pinned to the wall. He places them one by one into the unfocused collage of a large photomosaic.

He steps back, regards his work. The diving bird is a clutter of fractured stills; tail stretched, wings tucked into its body, beak touching the water as lightly as a kiss.

Thousands upon thousands of flawed fragments that, together, create a chaotic, flawless whole.

*

The man tidies the toys cluttering the stairs, loads the dishwasher, and sweeps the crumbs from under the dining table. He irons and folds the pile of washing, checks the windows, and locks the doors.

He turns out the lamp, lays a blanket over the little girl and, as he closes the curtains, watches the silhouette of a single bird drift across the convex crown of the moon. He smiles.

Maybe tomorrow.

Tin Can Phones

David O'Neill

Do you remember when you lived next door? With walls separated by a trickle of a lane, we talked through bruised and mottled tin cans. Your brother punctured holes, I found some string. We were close enough that an open window could carry our breath across but, to keep our words from the birds, we talked into the rattle and echo of aluminium.

I pictured your room as you described it, but your dad, the noisy one with the large fists, wouldn't let me upstairs so I was never sure. You saw my room though. My dad, the quiet one with the sad eyes and cloudy breath, wasn't around much.

I would eat my dinner fast enough to hurt then run upstairs, the cold of it pressed to my ear, waiting for the string to tighten with quick vibrations. We talked nothing like it meant everything. Once, something like heat bubbled right up to my teeth when you talked about a singer that was talented as well as cute. What is your favourite song? I should ask you that soon.

When my dad forgot to go back to work after lunch with the horses, we had to move across town. The houses were dustier and there was no lane between the walls, but the string was long enough. I had so much to tell you but I preferred to listen. The melody of your voice through that taut wire was the nicest thing in that house. I gathered up as much of it as possible and tried to keep it in a little piggy bank but it kept escaping through sellotaped cracks.

Mostly, you sounded happy, like you were two-stepping away from what went on downstairs, but sometimes, those shouts spilled into my ear too. I pretended not to hear them and asked you about that band. I knew when things were tough because my can would be quiet, empty, the string hanging limp across my carpet and I cried for you on those nights; big, bubbly hot ones. I never told you that though because men are supposed to have rocks and stones under their skin. My dad said things like that.

You told me that you were moving away; your mother was taking your brother and you to stay with her sister in some place you couldn't pronounce. I asked you to try so that I could find it on my map but it was torn in the important places so I asked you to come home soon instead. We held onto those cans that day and I watched as the thread grew thinner. Your voice still filled my room for a while and then nothing. I'm not sure how far you had travelled before it snapped.

I still talk to you. The can is a little rusted and bent out of shape from the time my dad stood on it by mistake but later, when I go upstairs, I will ask you about your favourite song.

Fog
Stuart Dybek

She kneels straddling his ankles, and he can feel her warmth and slickness as she slides up his shins, slowly working herself over the hump of his knees, along his thighs, up the entire length of his body. Not until she reaches his eyes does he close them. They are still closed when she lies back beside him and whispers, "I want you to carry away the smell of me."

That's how she says goodbye. Outside, her scent lingers as if it emanates as much from the misty night as from his skin— a scent already a secret, already a chill. He doesn't look up at her dark window from which, on other nights, she's watched him, her naked body wound in the drape. Tonight, a fine rain with the glitter of mica has paved the parking lot of the apartment complex where she lives, her mailbox and doorbell under a name other than her own. The name of a dead man. Above each doorway, the little orange bulbs beneath enamelled hoods are blurred.

Just last week this vapourish air would have crystallized into a late, last blizzard. Wet, weighty flakes would have coated the haloed, orange lamps, the parked cars, and empty streets in a luminescent white. Just weeks ago he was content to be immersed in winter, still the man he appeared to be, a man with his mind on weather as he waded out at night away from the bluish eye of a TV, carrying a sack of garbage through the lucid cold towards a trash can half-buried in a snow bank. He hadn't met her yet.

Headlights smoke. He drives surrounded by her scent, back towards the clarity of an unlit house still miles away, where a prior life waits patiently for his presence like a body awaiting its shadow, a dream awaiting a dreamer, a pew awaiting a penitent.

Fog drifts across the lake highway. Wipers can't sweep it aside. He wishes that he could vanish into it like red taillights.

Twenty-Five Seconds

David Steward

Watch. The image darkens and blurs, settles on its exposure and focus as he reaches the foot of the steps. Off screen, as if we were still together, I hear you breathe his name, in case I haven't seen him. He crosses the stage, swinging his arms, and turns a grin to someone near the front, where his class is sitting. There's a brief handshake, the clatter of applause, and the camera follows till he dips behind the heads of the audience.

I wanted to capture the moment, but as soon as it was over, I realised I'd been so intent on the little rectangular screen that I hadn't really seen him. It might have been better just to sit and watch, to take in the experience and hope it stayed with me. But that's the trouble: you can't rely on your memory to preserve a life of small, happy events. It's the moments of high emotion that come back to you: the humiliations and the rows, the separation.

Exactly the Way You Are

Nod Ghosh

Last night I dreamt Lorraine stole your underpants. The image of your wife smoothing silky fabric over her bottom was a quirk of my subconscious. She doesn't really wear Y-fronts.

Does she?

Your wife has changed though. She's more competitive and drives faster. Lorraine used to be placid. Now she argues like a politician, at least in my dreams.

Dream-Lorraine doesn't wear make-up. Gumboots have replaced strappy heels with diamante detail.

In my dreams, your wife has stopped shaving and has a moustache to rival Groucho Marx's. It's orangey-red, and matches the Velcro-short hair on her head.

Her voice is deep baritone.

In the dreams, Lorraine has quit orchestra and put her flute up on eBay.

She cuts thick yellow toenails and flicks shards onto the carpet, and scratches her crotch like she's contracted ringworm.

I've talked it through with Beverley. My wife reckons it's not Lorraine that's troubling me.

It's you.

The dreams have increased since I started feeling uneasy about the relationships we both have with each other's wives.

You and Bev used to go for a beer while Lorraine and I went to Zumba.

Now you don't communicate.

My recurring dreams invade daytime thoughts. I see Lorraine board a bus, a toolkit in her hand. I know she's not real. But then I see her pull out of the gas station in your truck and I'm less certain.

When Beverley and I visited last week, Lorraine wore peachy-gold eye shadow that picked out the highlights from her dress. Your wife told mine how well she looked. You weren't so civil. You said nothing to Beverley, like she was invisible or made of glass, brittle and dangerous to handle.

Lorraine sipped Sav Blanc while you drank lager. Beverley had cranberry juice as she was driving, and because she had a urinary infection.

Later, Beverley said she didn't want to visit anymore, couldn't take your coldness, though it would be a shame not to see Lorraine, she said. I said we won't go again and gave her a hug.

I can't stop dreaming about your wife. I know dream Lorraine and real Lorraine are different, just as real you and dream you are.

The dream-you is kind, though slow to adjust to changes in your dream-wife.

"One step at a time," you say.

In my dreams you're the brother I remember, the brother who looks out for your sister. You're courteous and supportive. You don't tell Lorraine how to dress or behave, like you tried with Beverley.

I'm proud of my dream brother. You love Lorraine. Your moustaches mingle when you kiss, red against brown.

There are no hypercritical comments.

There are no hypocritical comments.

Not like when *my* husband transitioned into a woman.

When I wake from those dreams, I miss the man-shaped Lorraine.

It's not that I don't like my sister-in-law exactly as she is. But in my dreams, she's married to a man whom I like exactly the way *he* is.

It's M.E., Not You

Matthew Thorpe-Coles

Katie's seemed a little bit down recently. She walks in everyday, heavy with the daily greys, sometimes wilting under the weekly shop. There's not much I can offer her anymore. I used to work fifty hour weeks, do the shopping and still have time to keep the house looking a bit less festered. One day I was living in a full sprint, the next my legs felt like they were trapped under sheets of prickled ice. Now I'm lucky if I can even get out of bed for more than two hours to offer her a cuppa and some motherly advice.

I do feel guilty for chucking her out into the world at fourteen, mind you. She's not the most confident of kids, and some of the other girls in her year make fun of her because she doesn't like to wear makeup. That's what she tells them anyway. I've seen her eyes when the glamorous celebrities come on the TV, and I know that if she didn't know how little money we get from my DLA, she'd have already asked for some makeup by now. But Katie gets on with life, doing all the housework I used to do, and I'm so proud of her for it. I know she rarely sees her friends, but we can't even afford her bus fare, and I often need her help getting up the stairs.

But today she looks depressed, and I can tell someone said something to her at school. She slumps on the sofa, her lips cracked from the cry she had before she got in. "A mother can always tell these things, Katie." I tell her, forcing myself from my chair and holding the crest of the sky above me, or so it feels.

"It's okay, Mum. They just… Took it too far today. Said I

was so ugly that I'd be better as a shut in, like they say you are." Katie replies, forcing a braced smile.

I smile back, and laugh "Just because I'm stuck inside, doesn't mean you have to be. It's me, not you remember, who's dealing with this. Besides, most of those girls have little rat-faces," Katie laughs at me, "and I'm saying that as your friend, not as your mother."

I make my way to my kitchen, pressing my eyes together so as not to cry. I may well be called a shut in, but my daughter didn't deserve to be. Reaching into my bag, I pull out my last £5 note. Money for the electric meter, normally, but Katie had less of an interest in TV recently, so it was going spare. At the bottom of my bag I spot a dark crimson lipstick, still there from my days working in a fierce office. I pluck it out, and bursting, I shout to Katie.

"Go get changed love, I've got a few things for you in here. You can go out with your friends tonight if you want."

Big Responsibilities

Megan Crosbie

He came home with us from the funfair, better than any stuffed animal or toffee apple. In the back seat of the car, I peered into the bag where he shimmered like treasure in the choppy glow of street-lights. I pressed my fingertips into the watery sack, trying to reach him.

We poured him into a mixing bowl and sat it on my desk. Mum promised we'd buy a proper fish tank in the morning. It was past bed time.

Drenched in darkness, the funfair still buzzed through me. I could smell it, as though wisps of candy floss were tangled around my nostrils and my bed swayed like a flying-saucer. I wondered if he felt homesick.

I tiptoed to him.

I watched from above as he swam circles, lost in the glass bowl, alone. He'd looked bigger in the bag, shifting his size between the ripples of plastic.

The water was colder on my hands than I'd expected. I grabbed around the glass curves, sloshing water onto my bare feet, until my fingers found his squirming body. I pulled him out and turned his surprised eyes to mine. He blew me kisses.

As I ran back to bed, I pressed him to my chest and he tried to swim into the damp patch in my nightie.

I placed him on my pillow and pulled the blanket up to our chins. I blew a kiss back, over the tiny waves of cotton between us. Dreamy thoughts lapped at the edges of my mind, as I felt him fall asleep beside me.

Breathing

Joanna Campbell

He never speaks when we drive to the station. He mutters, 'Bye, Dad,' as he climbs out, nothing more.

Every morning, I park close to the railings, not wanting to be in anyone's way, and watch him board the train. It's creepy, he says. An obsession. He gives it a series of initials that arch over me, an umbrella to stand beneath.

"There's a trend for it," he says.

"I've never been in fashion before," I tell him.

His laugh is like the rasp of a cracked nut that has disintegrated inside its shell.

I can't help it. Tucking the car under the drip of trees, I continue to wait. It goes back to when he slept as a baby and his mother would ask, "Is he still breathing?"

"Yes," I would reassure her, my head to his heart. "He's breathing."

He always chooses carriage B, the same seat. He stares ahead, although his eyes might turn in my direction. Hard to tell with the mist of my breath marshalling on the car window. I wait for the grasp of the wheels in their tracks before driving home.

He goes to his work and he comes home. He sits on a hard chair. Holds nothing in his hands. His friends gather dust. The spines of new books stay unbroken.

His mother would have searched for reasons. When he was three and we spotted he was left-handed, she said, "Where did he get that from, do you think?"

"Have you come down with a touch of something, do you think?" I ask him.

He says there is nothing. His eyes say the same.

"Not even something with initials?" I say, carelessly light-hearted, as if pressing him to take a whole biscuit from the muddle in the tin.

He changes to a carriage further along the track.

My wife whispers in my head, "Did he get in all right?" And I can't answer.

I clamber over the gearstick, across to the passenger seat, slide the window down. I strain my neck, but too much is in the way; the jolt and jerk of other doors, the press of passengers and smeared flanks of vending-machine, ticket-machine, hedges scrambling through the railings. But there is his hand, opening the door to carriage G.

Every day, there is his hand, the dark-brown suede of it. I bought the gloves for him one Christmas at the store where his mother and I shopped for presents when he was little. The year we bought his train-set, she hid the large plastic bag printed with a holly wreath. In the New Year, I found it, fastened with a headscarf round her neck, filled with her breath, a million clinging drops.

One day, his hand does not appear. Is he aboard?

"Is he still breathing?"

Old snow melts from the branches, dissolving on the ground in dark patches. And I tell her, this time I don't know.

'Let Robot Lawnmower Work. Enjoy Your Life!'

Danielle McLaughlin

The Callaghan girl took to calling round in the evenings when the lawnmower had finished its shift. She'd sit and stroke its hard-shelled back, her hair in those pigtails she should've outgrown, even allowing for her slow mind. She ought to be locked up, Victor said, when he saw her like that one evening, and I said she most likely would be some day.

A beetle that fed lustily on grass and weeds, on smaller beetles, ladybirds, and the occasional song thrush. That was what Robot Lawnmower resembled as it made its daily circuits, silently and without complaint. I won't deny that I came to know the precise times its schedule took it past the kitchen window. Or that on rainy days, when it couldn't leave its docking station, I was often gripped by a sense of being wholly alone.

There were other robot lawnmowers besides ours. At the Residents' Association meeting, Ben Timoney blushed and stuttered as he recounted how he'd discovered two in his back yard, one very still, the other moving against it, back and forth, back and forth, at an ever-quickening pace.

One Friday, when Victor was at bridge, when the Callaghans and their imbecile daughter were away, I lay down in the grass in front of Robot Lawnmower. His approach was as quiet as the parting of two blades of grass. I was a new frontier for him and he puzzled his way along my perimeters, retreating and advancing, nudging gently, before turning, eventually, to attend to a different section of garden.

The Residents' Association voted to ban robot lawnmowers. The secretary declared that there were many valid reasons for doing so—tripping hazards, their unsettling effect on dogs— without the need to record in the minutes the things Ben Timoney had spoken of. The woman from the bungalow on the corner got to her feet, said that they would have to take her first. An amendment was proposed, seconded, passed to say that the ban applied to future acquisitions only.

One night, I woke to a low, rumbling sound. I parted the curtains to see the Callaghan girl coming down the street, pulling a suitcase on wheels. Her hair was loose of its pigtails. Behind her were a dozen or more robot lawnmowers, their pace and formation suggesting funeral procession, or presidential cavalcade, or both. I rushed outside, discovered ours gone from its docking station. By the time I reached the front gate, they were level with our house. 'Thief!' I shouted at the Callaghan girl. She stopped. Though I'd always presumed her mute, she said: I have nothing that belongs to you. She walked on, the lawnmowers gliding after her. I watched for ours as they passed, thinking to snatch it up, but beneath the street lamps they all shone gold, gilded scarab beetles that might grace a giant neck, changed utterly, unrecognisable.

The Skirt

Sophie van Llewyn

The year when the Beloved Leader came to our town, my mother didn't cook us dinner for eleven days in a row. The Beloved Leader had to inaugurate a truck factory and my mother was tailoring a skirt from dark red tweed.

The skirt was meant to be tight at the top and flaring at the bottom, ending at knee level. Something must have gone wrong, because my mother had to undo it after six days and start again. After that, she barely spoke to me. She went around the house with the measuring tape draped around her neck like a necklace, pins stuck in her collar.

The day after the skirt was done, my teacher came to school wearing it. The folds had a liquid quality about them, shifting with every motion. Two days later, on the day that the nominations for the position of flower bearer were made, my teacher was wearing the skirt again. When the moment came, she called my name and my classmates applauded. It was the greatest honour imaginable: coming close to the Beloved Leader, giving him flowers.

At home, my mother and I practised the act of bestowing.

A week later, a lady with a purple hat from the Party came to inspect all candidates. The nominees were rounded up in the school festivity hall.

We went up on stage in groups of six, where she would ask us to smile, turn, walk and pretend that we were giving flowers. When it was my turn to perform, she leaned in closer. She smelled of tobacco, coffee and a Bulgarian rose perfume my aunt also used to wear. She asked me if my eyes were mismatched. I informed her that I had a grey eye and a brown eye.

The lady wrinkled her nose. It didn't occur to me to explain that there were many mismatched things in my life. For instance, my mother's expectations.

My mother asked me how it went. When I told her, her lips tightened as if a magic string had been pulled through their flesh and someone was tugging hard at it.

That spring, the Beloved Leader came and I was not there to give him flowers.

For the remainder of the school year, we dined in silence and I didn't lift my offending eyes from the plate.

On The Way Out

Erica Plouffe Lazure

The Way Out! was the one ride at the carnival guaranteed to topple your stomach, to bend and wail your oesophagus, to feel your gut in your throat, and only a steady scream would keep down the hot dogs and spun floss. Our mothers let us ride because they trusted the strap-in safety belts, trusted the system would keep us safe. It gave us our wild, ten-minute ride of topsy and turvy and a guaranteed return to our mothers, and in time we'd become the responsible adults the current ones needed us to someday become because "Who's gonna wipe our ass?" they'd joke. "Not me!" we'd reply. "Not yet!" And so when the carnival power lines cut that night, leaving us stranded mid-scream, newly free of inertia, our bodies suspended in the tiny tin box, for the first time we saw the world below us dark and still save for the few glowing generator-fed lights, the stumbling clusters of fairway bodies, and we began to cry for our mothers, cried to bring the power back, to be free, to be on the ground away from the darkened horizon. "Who's gonna come for us?" one of us said, palms pressed against her now floating skirt, and another cried "Satan!" and all within earshot screamed in the dark on the tip top of the longest arm in the tiny tin box, each of us clutching our seat belts, sniffling tears down our throats.

And when the power returned, some 10 minutes later, you could feel the current surge on the air, as each light glint its calliope glow red then blue then green then red again, and the vendors settled back into selling the bagged spun floss and the hot dogs, and the din of eighty different melodies hovered above the tents, and our tin box on The Way Out! lifted with all of it, its stiff electric arm arcing us slowly, reluctantly, back to earth.

Vacation Dog

Pamela Painter

The first photo of our boxer appeared with our dog sitter's text *Couldn't pass up chance 2 see Grand Canyon. Will take good care of Philco.* So, there is Annie with Philco standing against the red rust backdrop of the western-most part of the Canyon. Annie is smiling emoji-like into her guy's camera, Philco's leash tightly wound around her forearm, his tongue lolling out in Philco-joy. My husband, George, snorts in annoyance when I show him the photo and goes back to pawing through his mother's desk for checkbooks, bills, any uncashed stock certificates. He insisted I accompany him to Seattle to help clear out her ten-room house and has relegated me to silver, china, and her collection of glass animals, as if I didn't know he's been bringing his intern, Isabelle, here for the past three months. She probably chose the guest room's garish sheets, scattered the candles here and there, and forgot to step back into the purple silk triangle of thong, peeking out from under the bed. Annie's next photo has all three, Annie, Philco, and her guy drinking tequila in the back of his red pick-up, a floppy tent with scraggly trees in the background. George says he hopes Philco isn't returned to us with ticks or fleas. I've been hoping to avoid an STD. The texts and photos keep coming as if to assure us that the kidnapped—dog-napped—Philco is still alive. Philco catching a Frisbee. Philco asleep on his back. Philco peeing on a yucca plant, about to get a needle in his back paw. I save each photo and follow their canyon tour on line. Three days later, I plan a trip of my own and leave for home where I will pack up George's study, plow his clothes into garbage bags, file for divorce. Philco will be home from his vacation by then. That's what it took: me jealous of Philco. Imagine: jealous of a dog.

Swing State

Claire Polders

It's useless to worry about the future, I remember my father saying. *Imagine fretting about the dentist all week and then the appointment is cancelled.* We're in the abandoned backyard of a house up in the Swiss mountains. Alone and together. Leftovers of last night's campfire lie blackened on the darkening grass. It's the end of the day. I sit down on the tree swing—if I'm too old to be swinging, I make it a point not to care. I get myself started, step backward, and let go. Do you see me flying? On my third sway, my father pushes me gently toward the dying light. The air is soft. I oscillate. The clouds in the evening sky are only on the horizon, at a distance, glowing red. Away from his hands, on the weightless moment at the top of the arc, I turn my head and catch a glimpse of him. His sad face in the twilight has an unfamiliar quality. He's much younger than the last time I saw him. Falling down, my lower back meets his hands again, which are now cold. With eyes closed, I see his still body on the wooden bed, lips glued, hands wrinkled like those of an old man. My father's push and gravity's pull. In between, for long uplifting seconds, I'm present between past and future, suspended in air. Then the sun goes down as if forever.

Happiness

Paul Currion

Happiness is a garishly coloured parrot that sits on his shoulder and squawks in his ear all day long, providing a running commentary on how great everything is. When he can't stand any more, he tries to grab it by the neck; but it simply topples off his shoulder and flaps around the room, easily evading his clutches.

As soon as he gives up, it flies back to the same perch and takes up its recital again. "That sunset is just amazing! Things are going well for you at work this year. Mmm, that burrito was a good choice. You know, these Sunday mornings really are a special time."

He hates the parrot. He hears what it's saying, and he agrees with almost everything (although he wasn't entirely sure about that burrito), but he just doesn't... feel it. He knows that he'll always have to carry the parrot, and he knows that he'll never get used to it, and he knows that nobody else will ever understand.

He's absolutely certain about all these things right up to the moment when he sees a girl standing on the far side of the room at a party, staring at him.

No! She's not staring at him, but at his parrot, watching it very carefully as if she can't believe her eyes. Here's what's really strange: his parrot has stopped squawking. He turns his head to look at it – completely silent, completely still, as if it's been stunned by the sun – and realises that it's staring back at the girl.

He looks back and meets her gaze for the first time, and

smiles. It's only then that he realizes that his parrot isn't looking at her at all; it's looking at the identical parrot that sits on her shoulder: completely silent, completely still.

Who Came?

Calum Kerr

Frank sat on the bench and gazed out across the lake. There was only slight breeze to ruffle the water, and disturb the perfect reflection of the blue sky and the black flecked birds, the trees on the far bank and hills that upstaged them.

Perhaps it would be better to call it a loch. Or une lac. The thought floated through his head, but didn't land.

He seemed to have been sitting here for an age, but he had lost track of time so very long ago.

Finally, he heard the noise he had been waiting for – the brush of cloth against leaf, the tread of shoe on shore.

He didn't look around until he felt the bench shift under him with the addition of new weight.

"Davey," he said.

The other man looked at him. "Frankie," he replied.

They held each other's gaze, serious looks on their faces. But after only a few seconds, Frank could no longer hold it and broke into a grin. The pair laughed as they hugged.

"So, you're dead then," Frank commented, after they had composed themselves.

"Yep."

"Was it bad?"

"I don't remember really. The last year or two was all a bit cloudy. Dementia. You know."

Frank gave a slow nod. "A blessing, then."

"Yeah."

They fell silent for a moment.

106

Then, "So?" Frank asked.

"What?" Dave tore his gaze from the hypnotic horizon.

"Are you going to tell me?"

Dave gave him a look of incomprehension, which after a moment dissolved into a smile. "I thought maybe you'd forgotten."

"I was hit by a bus, not by the stupid-stick like you. Come on!"

Dave looked away, drinking in the view for another few moments, teasing his friend as the moment dragged out.

"Dave!" Frank's voice was half-threat/half-whine.

Finally, his friend relented. "There were loads of them. All the guys – of course. The family – of course."

"And?"

Dave nodded. "Yep, they were all there. All in black. Every one of the old girls."

"All of them?"

"Well, apart from Maureen, because…"

"Yeah, because of that bloody bike." He looked off into space. "Wow. So a good turnout, then?"

"Bloody good, I thought."

"Tears?"

"Yep."

"Beers?"

"Of course."

Frank nodded, and gave a sigh. "That's good."

The two men lapsed into companionable silence, and stared out across the water. The wind had gathered pace and the surface was alive with sparkling ripples.

"So, what now?" Dave asked, after a while.

Frank shrugged. "I suppose we have to wait for Derek to come and tell us how yours was."

"If he can remember. I think he was getting a bit gaga too."

"Oh well, we'll see," replied Frank.

Living Alone with Derrida

Zoe Murdock

I was twenty-five, recently divorced, and living alone for the first time in my life. I signed up for classes at the university and rented a little furnished apartment on a circling street that always led me straight back to where I'd started, which was exactly how my life had been going up to that point.

The apartment was full of white hair. It was in the carpets and on the headrest of the orange recliner. I thought it was cat hair, but then I realized it was human hair from that old couple who lived in the apartment before me. It wasn't gross, just a curious feature of my new solitary confinement.

I was taking a class on the French philosopher, Derrida, and since the apartment was cold and dark, I'd take my book outside and sit in the sun in the driveway to read. Derrida's philosophy was hard to understand, but it seemed like he was saying that even though I thought I knew what I was saying with my words, that wasn't really true. The problem was, once my words entered the world, their meaning was filtered through the unique experience and understanding of each person who heard or read them. At that point they didn't really belong to me anymore.

The more I read, the more I realized the meaning of my words had never been my own. Their meaning had come from people who taught me how to say and write them. And yet they were the basis of my beliefs. Beliefs about gender. Patriotism. Religion.

I thought about all that as I wandered around my little apartment picking up white hairs. If my words weren't my own, and yet they defined me, how could I really know who I was?

A few weeks later, I met a psychology student. He started coming around, and my apartment got a lot brighter. The bed got a lot smaller, and cosy. I talked to him about Derrida, and then he informed me that we were all just products of behavioural conditioning. That my parents and teachers, and everyone else I knew, had made me into who I was by how they had punished or praised me. The idea scared me and then I got mad. I had already learned about the controlling power of words, and now this. Did I have any free will at all?

It disturbed me to think I wasn't my own person. That I had somehow been constructed by words and the people around me. I was determined to do something about it, even if I had to deconstruct myself.

Then, the Spring rain came. It melted the snow in the mountains so fast the water roared down into the city, wiping out everything in its way. It brought down old trees that had been there for years, completely changing the landscape. It felt like the anger and confusion had escaped my mind and entered the world. It was a scary idea, but by then, I was starting to like scary.

Tenders

Meg Pokrass

He said to meet him in the Tenders & Muffins at lunchtime, that he couldn't say why, which made as much sense as the fact that cat urine glows in the dark, which it does. I pulled out my phone to see if he had texted, but he hadn't. My phone looked like the cockpit of a plane, and I understood how to make it do hundreds of wonderful things. It was the only object I loved and trusted.

At lunch, the waitress came over and looked at me hard, as if I'd just been playing with somebody's dick—women looked at me with anger more than I could understand, I always smiled at them, but people are animals and none of us get why we hate each other.

He sat down and said he was very hungry.

"Thank you, thank you, thank you, thank you for coming here," he said.

"Did you see anyone else from production? Is anyone from production here?" he asked.

I loved his belly, and wanted to take off my shoes so I could warm my toes on it.

"Nope," I said. "Nope, nope."

"I'm going to tell you too much now," he said, then signaled the mean-eyed waitress and ordered two Polar Bear sandwiches and one garlic fry plate. "We can share," he said.

"I would like that," I said, wishing I had brought my Emetrol, which makes me feel all cozy and taken care of instead of nauseous and bad. The urge to pee was knocking or was it nausea, sometimes it all felt the same. I could see he wanted, no, he needed, all my attention.

It was time to say something that would fix him. Why did smells bother me so much?

"How tiny..." he said, looking at my folded hands, his face pinking from hunger, or from lust, or from depression. He knew that I went to three meetings a day in three different neighborhoods so I wouldn't have much time for small talk, and this was something we shared. There seemed to be a magnet between us, stuck and pretty.

I looked at my hands, and they had veins like my grandmother's hands.

The waitress asked us if we would be ordering dessert. I said we would split a hot fudge Sunday with whipped cream and nuts. She smirked and nodded. In the bar I could tell what the movie was, it was the one where people became flies and killed each other.

On the Track You Tasted Blue

Anne Summerfield

You turned a nut along the length of a bolt, lying on your back reaching up. A small operation like twisting a bottle top, over and over until your whole body throbbed and at midday break you could hardly ease the cheese and pickle on white from the sandwich tin your wife had bought you. The coffee spilled when you tried to pour it from tartan flask. You mopped it up with your sleeve before you sipped the drink through its oily shimmer. One of the other men gave you sugar to put in it, though you'd given sugar up, and then he gave you a fag which you'd also given up and you went outside to see daylight and breathe in air heady with paint fumes.

'That tastes like blue,' the bloke beside you said, and you thought of green. It was the first job you'd had indoors. Then it was time to go back to the track and turn nuts down bolts for four hours, maybe more, until the whistle blew and you and all the others in blue overalls with pieces of Mini Coopers in your pockets could clock out and carry your empty lunchboxes home.

The Most

Etgar Keret

When I was little, my Mom had only one fear — that I'd grow up to be ordinary.

Our family, as everyone knows, has been ordinary going back four generations. Really nice, but so normal you could die. And my Mom wasn't going to let me end up like that too.

That's why, from the day I was born, she and my Dad saved their pennies, and when I was 12, they sent me to the International Boarding School for the Fostering of Excellence in Switzerland.

The International Boarding School placed a very strong emphasis on achievement and uniqueness, and its graduates were known the world over for excellence in their fields. The fields themselves didn't matter to the administration as long as the child excelled at them. In my class, for example, Caroline was studying to be the most beautiful, and Raul was already the most obnoxious and constantly hassled Yu-Lin, who was the most pathetic.

The teacher seated me at a desk with someone whose name nobody knew, but one quick look at him was enough to see that he was the kid who wanted the most. No one knew what he wanted, because he never spoke. But his eyes were open really wide, trying to see, and his tongue was always waving around in his mouth, as if it was tasting something not there, and that golf ball in his throat went up and down every few seconds the way it does when you swallow.

If I'd known what that kid wanted, I would have killed for him to have it. But I didn't and neither did the teachers. They didn't even try to find out — it was enough that he excelled at wanting it.

So I spent a whole year staring at the kid without a name. A year during which Caroline had a cheekbone transplant and Yu -Lin tried to kill herself twice.

We were considered a very successful class, except for me and maybe Raul, who occasionally disappointed with uncontrollable displays of niceness. In a desperate attempt to show his commitment, Raul killed our biology teacher. But as the pedagogical advisors told his parents, it was too little too late, and we were both expelled.

The charter flight home was unpleasant. I knew my parents would still love me, but I was afraid of their disappointment when they found out what I always knew — that I was just like everyone else.

No one spoke on the way home from the airport, and when we arrived, it was already dark. Mom looked at the bags of frozen vegetables in the fridge and asked in a choked voice whether I wanted anything. I closed my eyes and knew I wanted. I wanted something. Without a name, but with a smell and a taste. I didn't want it the most, not half as much as that kid who sat next to me at school, but for me, it was somehow enough.

Translated by Sondra Silverston

Originally published online at Electric Literature as 'My Time at the International Boarding School for the Fostering of Excellence' (https:// electricliterature.com/my-time-at-the-international-boarding-school-for-the-fostering-of-excellence-new-fiction-by-etgar-e0110d017117#.jwengs6g2)
© 2015, Etgar Keret The Seven Good Years by Etgar Keret is published by Granta. http://etgarkeret.com/

Fascinate

Judy Darley

I still remember the April when we were small and found a nest of ducklings in a hanging basket. We climbed up on the kitchen roof and scooched close to stare at them.

"Ducklings are magic, Helen," you told me. "They're so light and fluffy they can survive a fall from any height."

You reached out and scooped one into your palm before I could stop you. It sat there, the breeze weaving through its downy feathers. Then, grinning, you launched it with force into the air. It splatted against the flagstones below with a squelch that rang through my head. You blinked at me, and giggled.

"Oops. Don't tell!" And you slithered off the roof, kicking the tiny corpse beneath the rhododendron leaves where no one would see.

Now we're grown and sensible, but you're still my kid sister, even if you are about to be married.

You tasked me with booking the hen party. "Something cool," you said. "Something none of the hens will ever forget."

When I spotted the craft-ti-dermy classes, I knew I'd found the right thing, even if the thought of it made me feel a bit sick inside.

Taxidermy for a new generation – desiccated chicks, mice and birds decorated with sequins and stitched into fascinators.

"Helen, it's perfect!" you squeaked as we settled down to get to work with tweezers and thread. The other hens murmured politely, loathe to own up to the horror wriggling through them.

Choosing a creature was a challenge. I watched you paw through the cadavers. "Is there a kitten?"

The course leader explained that people don't like to dismantle cats or dogs – the trend for ghoulish doesn't reach quite that far. I suppose they have to draw the line somewhere, or some bride, somewhere, will be gliding down an aisle with a baby's sweet feet curling coquettishly on her tiara.

In the end you opted for a starling, killed by a collision with a plate glass window.

I chose the smallest thing in the heap – a frog murdered by dehydration. All had died of natural causes, none raised and slaughtered for this purpose, we were assured.

We slit stomachs, removed innards, inserted miniature glass eyes like gems.

At last the torture ended. Your fascinator was a triumph; the wings outspread as though taking flight.

On the day of your wedding I watched the sky for murmurations, and wondered whether I'd speak up if one appeared.

Legs in the Air,
We Think about Spring

Angela Readman

There were no bouquets the day they buried the master. Crows followed the ploughs and ate from the furrows. I didn't know who would come after so long, but the church wasn't empty. The pews were lined with girls he had mentored. Though we were old now, and the only sign we were ever his was the way we fiddled with our handkerchiefs.

I looked down and saw I'd folded a windmill. A woman near-by made a hymn sheet into a swan. We saw one other and nodded: Yes, the master taught us well, his lessons lived in our fingers still.

No one in the world could fold as well as that man. Not just paper, which he made into animals, furniture, cities, but people. He could find a girl hiding under a bed and show her how to be anything. He took on several apprentices each year. He always knew an origami girl, he said. They were small. They carried themselves like unopened letters. There was precision in the way certain chambermaids made a bed, or opened a purse. He spotted servers folding napkins looking sorry they couldn't do more.

We followed the priest single-file to the graveside. The women were silent, no one allowed a single tear to slide down her face. It was as if we were still in the bottle, aware of the impact our slightest move had on our surroundings. The act was the pinnacle of our careers. When the master lectured about letting go of the limits of skin and bone, he brought out the bottle with a girl inside like a message at sea.

In there, the world was muffled and shining. Our breath was clouds. We made kissy faces and saw our lipstick under glass like butterflies. It was where we found love, even the plain girls, as if there was no pretty or ugly in the bottle, just a person folded into shape. I met my husband that way, lots of us did. Quietly, we watched them breathe on glass and write their names in reverse. Once we'd mastered the bottle, most of us retired.

No husbands accompanied us now. We came to bid farewell to the master alone, grief uncurling quiet as holly in our throats. They lowered the casket and we looked down, expecting the body to fold the soil into a crane. When it didn't, we looked up. The sun pleated the clouds. The day looked like it wanted to be lighter, but didn't know how. The fields were bare.

'There are no flowers,' someone said. She lay on her back and lifted her legs, and we followed. Women lay on the grass—propped on our shoulders, heads like bulbs, legs stalks bursting from the ground. From the road, anyone could see our skirts falling, feet pointing buds, all of us trying to be irises, lilies, laid on our backs for that final beautiful trick no one had taught us yet.

The Boy at a London Bus Stop Who Took My Photograph in the Summer of 1999

Anna Nazarova-Evans

I stepped over it. I didn't pick up the toy that toddler had dropped on the floor. Rushed past him. Why didn't I pick it up?

Many years ago, as I was starting university, a guy came up to me at a bus stop. He asked to take my picture for a photography project. Underneath it, he wanted to include my answer to the following question:

"If you could say something to the whole world – what would you say?"

I got embarrassed because the guy was cute and mumbled something awfully stupid about make up.

"Are you sure?" he said. "That would be your one message to the whole entire world?"

"I don't know, I really don't know!" I panicked.

I was seventeen. He put me on the spot. If only I met him now.

In the last year of my degree one of the lecturers got very irate with me taking notes on my laptop because of the tapping noise the keys made. She insisted that I take written notes, which I thought to be very rude at the time. I showed my displeasure by making snide remarks about her behind her

119

back with other students, which she eventually figured out. It was yesterday that I found out that high irritability to mild sound pollution is a tell-tale sign of M.E.

The girl I interviewed for a job once walked in in heels so high, she couldn't unbend her knees. Her skin was covered up thick, like papier-mâché. She hardly took up any space at all. She leant on my desk with a bony elbow and I fell in love. She was awkward and terrible at her job, so I couldn't hire her, but I thought of her every day, even after my wedding. I often thought—what if I was the only person to ever see her in that light? I prayed that someone would see me like that, even if I never found out about it. It was wonderful to know that this feeling existed.

When my husband died at the age of forty-four, the dog greeted me with wet eyes every night for months. I came home from work, thinking on inertia that he was on his way back too. Every time it was a shock to find her whimpering and burrowing her face in the cushions on his side of the bed. At first I tried to explain to her that he was not coming back, that she must stop waiting. I tried to reason with an Alsatian. But then I gave up and cried and howled and whimpered with her, until he let go of both of us.

That time at the bus stop, the guy told my seventeen-year-old self that later in life I would think back to that moment and I would regret it.

He was right.

They Keep Calling My Ex-Husband Brave

Santino Prinzi

His friends, his parents, his colleagues. My friends, my parents, my colleagues. Whenever I ask *What makes him so brave?* they answer with scowls and accusations. You aren't the victim here. They keep telling me he could've lost everything. Me, the very person who has. Have sympathy. Empathise. *Unless you've been there, Esme, you have no right to say anything.*

I haven't been there, but I am here, I haven't lost my voice. Nobody's asked me if I'm okay.

His act of "bravery" replays in my mind again and again and again the way Lindy watches *Tangled*. Him: he's sitting over the kitchen table, hunched over, his face in his hands, crying. Me: confused, trying to comfort him, trying to get him to tell me what's wrong. Him: he wipes his blotchy face, inhales, *I'm*—his words catch in his throat. Me: I'm crumbling under the weight of the questions I want to ask. *How long have you known? What about our daughter? What about us? Did you ever love me?* He tells me it's difficult for him, and I scream *It's difficult for me too!* We sit in silence, then he leaves.

Tears. Divorce. Moving boxes; mine, not his. Too young to understand, Lindy wants to stay with Daddy, and does. With him and his new friend Murphy, who has everything I wanted, everything I worked for. How long had he and my husband known each other? I assess every moment we shared,

121

everything he said. All of my husband's friends are subject to re-evaluation. There's nothing more I want than to think about something else, to think—about—something—else—tothinkaboutsomethingelse!

My therapist says I'm not homophobic for believing my husband isn't brave, which isn't what everyone else tells me. His ex-wife left him for another woman. *Fascinating*, he tells me, but I don't see how. He reminds me that *He didn't reject you, he rejected your gender. It's not the same.* But it doesn't explain. It doesn't explain—anything.

After visiting Lindy, and *them*, my parents tell me he's much happier now. *Really, he's come into his own; it's like he's been reborn.* I want to shake them. I want to shake them all so hard again and again and again until they understand. Until they get it.

He didn't reject you, he rejected your gender. It's not the same.
    But I'm yet to see the difference.

Carousel

Judi Walsh

I once watched a TV programme about how orcas catch fish. They are known as killer whales, and they live up to their name. They conspire to herd the herring into a ball, to force them up to the air, where they can't breathe. Each orca dives underneath the ball, calling to its friends, flashing its white belly to disarm the fish. They kill them with beauty. They blow tiny bubbles, strings of deathly diamonds, which force the terrified herring closer and closer in a transparent noose. Once the herring are at the surface, jumping like they are already in the boiling pot, one killer whale slaps its tail as if to say "dinner's ready!" and they all eat the exploding feast.

Killer whales are really dolphins, and they are very intelligent. We can learn a lot from the way they behave. Here is what I have learned. Be on your guard. Don't get caught. There is no safety in numbers. Do not accept gifts from strangers, no matter how much they sparkle. Do not lay meekly showing your own belly because they show you theirs.

How Traveller Boys Love

Lindsay Fisher

Don't nobody love me like Mickey does. Don't never need to say it. I just know. Like when we is up at the river and he shows me where the fish is sleeping close into the bank and he takes my hand and he leads me to a brown trout there. He tickles it under its white belly and slowly lifts it nearer the surface so I can see. It's like he's showing me his heart, and it kicks then, tail and fin, twisting its whole fish-body in a rainbow commotion, and I get it.

Mickey just laughs and he looks at me and I laugh, too, and the brown trout breaks the water, then is gone down into the cold deep dark. Mickey says my name, like maybe that's the name of the fish, and he says it wistful, like he wishes it would swim back to his hand. I lean in and kiss him, fish-wet kisses, and I say his name back to him.

Mickey holds me close under the stars and the moon. And the smoke from a wood-fire is in his hair and on his clothes. I breathe him in, all bitter and sweet. And I know he will always love me and love me like no other.

I've been with other boys and they is all running hands and blowing air and hard cocks pressing 'gainst me through their clothes. And they is so taken up with their own breathlessness that they don't even see me – I could be any girl in that touching dark. After, when they is done and I wipe my hand on the grass, they see me then, and it's not love that's in their eyes or their words.

With Mickey it's different. He's got all sorts of respect for me. He blesses me with his words, and his kisses are not hungry, and he touches my neck and my hair and my cheek, touching gentle as birdwing or moth. And he lays all his secret wonders before me, and there's such love in that.

There's an egg-filled nest in the ragged privet hedge that runs along one side of Duthie park. It's a robin's nest, he says, and three hen-speckled blue-sky eggs, warm as breath in my cupped hand, and he says we must be quick or the robin will know — worse yet, the boys'll know, the cock-sure boys that have names for us and those names sharp as thrown stones and they don't ever leave us alone.

And Mickey takes me to a box of bees that's out on the far edge of a field and we watch the to-ing and fro-ing, listening to the sound of 'em, which is like music when it has no words and is simply humming. And he dares brave their stings to fetch me a broke bit of comb with sweet honey dripping. And Mickey don't never have to tell me he loves me, for it's there in everything he does.

The Complete and Incomplete Works of Lydia Davis

Ingrid Jendrzejewski

When we began to write again in earnest, we wrote about the usual things: our relationships, our children, grammar, insects, becoming trees. We were reasonably happy with our work; if nothing else, it was precisely punctuated.

Most of what we wrote was short, and, as we discovered when we began to look for places to send it, much of it did not sit nicely within convenient genre categories. We did not know whether to address our submissions to the poetry editor, the fiction editor, the non-fiction editor, all three at once, or – as we began to suspect as the rejection notices amassed – none at all. Still: we kept writing, we kept editing, we kept submitting, and we believe we felt that we were making some sort of modest progress.

Then, there came the day when we chanced upon an article about Lydia Davis in the *New Yorker*, a magazine we read voraciously in our teens, not at all in our twenties and on occasion now that we have children. It is unusual, these days, for us to make time to read a long article about an author with whom we are not familiar, however, for some reason, we read the article about Lydia Davis. We were not sure, from just reading the article, that we would like Lydia Davis' writing, but we found ourselves ordering a collection of her complete works, which we then read from start to finish in a short amount of time.

As we read, we became more and more alarmed. In this

collection, we found versions of all the short pieces that we had tried to write in the past year – at least, all the pieces with which we were most satisfied – and these versions were much better than ours. We could not find any ground in our own writing that Lydia Davis had not already surveyed and claimed. We could not think of any ground that we wanted to cover over which Lydia Davis had not already trod. Lydia Davis' fingers had been in all the pies before we had even known that there were pies to be had. We found it all rather uncanny.

After reading Lydia Davis, we found writing difficult. We tried to think of things of which Lydia Davis would not think, and write about them in ways in which Lydia Davis would not write. However, our attempts to escape Lydia Davis in our writing made Lydia Davis all the more present. She loomed over our shoulders, and roared every time we tried to commit a word to paper.

For a time, we were silenced. But then, it occurred to us that perhaps we were not us after all, but actually something created by Lydia Davis: one of her various selves. After much analysis, this seemed the most plausible explanation of us and our writing. We try to content ourselves with this knowledge, but we lack grace and often fail.

Ana and Jose-Ramon

Jason Jackson

When they were children, Ana and Jose-Ramon used to chase chickens. Once, he grabbed a black one by the neck, ripped the head right off.

"*Mira!*" he laughed. "Look!" He was covered in blood, and he threw the dead thing—still twitching—at Ana as she ran from him.

But soon they were chasing chickens again.

Time, as it does in any village, passed slowly, but eventually Jose-Ramon married a stupid, beautiful girl called Rosa and soon there were children. Six, seven. Ana could never tell. More time passed, and each child left the village as soon as they were grown.

Ana never married, never took a lover. She was too plain. Too strong.

"Perhaps," said her father, "you're just scared." Her mother had died on the birthing table, and her father would often tell her about the blood. One morning, she took him his *café con leche* and he was cold, his eyes wide. She pulled on her boots and walked into the village to fetch the doctor, all the while thinking how there was really no need.

People were surprised that she kept the farm, but it was her life. "It's all I know," she would say, and that would seem to answer them. She employed local girls to help, and some even enjoyed the work. Jose-Roman would come over often, say "You want to sell me this place?" He liked *patatas bravas, jamón.* He would sit in the kitchen, boots off, drinking *aguardiente* while she cooked. "I'm glad I never married you, Ana. My wife is stupid, but *Dios!* What a body!"

The village mourned when Jose-Ramon's wife died, but Ana worked the day of the funeral. It was best not to pretend.

Soon she heard tales. Jose-Ramon's chickens were running loose. Candles burned at his windows all night.

His door was open when she arrived, and he was drunk, sitting in a chair, naked.

She looked him in the eye, said, "If things are still this bad in a month, I will take this place from you."

Within a few days the chickens were penned, and there were no candles burning through the night. Sometimes she would hear from people in the village that he was well, that he was sober, but he never came around anymore.

Finally, she took her father's shotgun from the cupboard, and she headed out into the cool evening.

Jose-Ramon opened his door in his nightshirt. His skinny legs. His hair awry. This old man who had once pulled the heads from chickens!

She prodded the gun at him. "If I am to die a virgin, it will be by my own hand, tonight, and I will die a murderess too."

Jose-Ramon looked at her for a long time, but he smiled when he said, "Ana, you'll have no need of the gun."

Weather Girl

Robert Shapard

They said she'd gone to Virginia to be the weather girl for a TV station. I don't think so. I saw her tangled in the weather balloon. I saw it swept up in the storm. There's no way she could survive. The line was doubled around her waist, everybody screaming and scrambling. I saw the look of terror in her eyes. Then the squall ripped her away, gusting over the campus lagoon, shooting skyward in a lane of sun, imagine the power of it, in barely a minute the balloon was just a bright silver pin between massive storm clouds over the Gulf. We all saw it on TV the next day, where it landed hundreds of miles away deflated and mangled across a Pensacola gas station like a giant condom.

I'd had a feeling when she turned up in our program a few days before she wasn't long for us. The way she talked about isobars and air masses, it was poetry not data points. Me, I can read charts is about all. The night before the storm I asked her, Why are you here? It was a big party and she shouted, What? I repeated and she touched my face and shouted in my ear she'd been lonely in her room. Then she said, You're sweet! I said, No, I mean, what are you doing in a little coastal Florida college program like this? She made a pouty face and said, Stanford didn't want me. We drank too much and I asked her to sleep with me. The next morning I thought she had. Her scent was everywhere, on my t-shirt, in my head. I was late for the balloon launch, the squall was coming in, everybody was screaming, and she was dancing around trying to get untangled. She saw me running. For an instant she got this calm look of resignation that said goodbye, I could have loved you. Then she was gone.

The rest of the day I kept saying we've got to find her. People were confused. They said everybody's accounted for, but she *wasn't*. In the department they said she'd *never enrolled.*

I called Uncle Bob in Port St. Joe the next night. I said, I don't know if this is for me. What kind of college is it where a girl is lost in a storm and nobody even *acknowledges* it? I kept seeing her in that cut off tee and those jeans with her knees showing. Uncle Bob had told me before I should go in the Coast Guard because they always need climatologists. It was hot, I under a campus streetlamp sweating, bugs whirling around me. I guess I broke down. I said Jesus, sometimes I just want to sail away forever. Uncle Bob was quiet a moment. You're young, he said. I don't think he understood what I was saying. It's a good program, he said. People are always gonna need fishing forecasts.

The Way We Lie

KM Elkes

I get the best dreams lying on my right side. Don't ask me why. When I roll the other way, so that I'm facing the wall, I don't get the same quality. Trouble is the good way faces my husband. Now he's a hefty guy, so I start to roll into the pit he's making in the bed. And I like to tuck the duvet under my chin to achieve the best conditions for dreams. But that's difficult, logistically speaking, because when I'm facing the right way, the duvet goes up like a big surf swell over my husband.

Even when I do get things just so, he often turns so we're face-to-face. I don't like him breathing on me. That's when I spin and face the wall and say 'so long' and 'sayonara' to my best dreams.

I tell my husband all about this one morning. We're at the age when we wake early (though there's absolutely no need) and take a coffee in bed before we go to work.

When I finish, he just says: "That's not what I see, baby."

"How do you know what I do, you're always asleep?"

"Am I?" he says. "Last night you were on your right side and your legs were churning like you were running hard. And your teeth were grinding. Was that a good dream?"

I take a sip of coffee. He does make good coffee. I can't actually remember any of the details of my dreams. But that's beside the point.

"I just feel like they are better. Something happens in them. They're more colourful."

"But you say you don't remember them? Yep, that makes sense."

He gets up. I notice, not for the first time, that he needs new underpants. They are baggy. Everything he wears is baggy. Everything gets baggy when you get older.

He starts to do the stretches for his back. I watch him straining to touch his toes.

"Want to know something else?" he says. "You moan when you are sleeping on your right side. Moan like a ghost. It's terrible. I flip you so you point the other way."

"That's stopping my good dreams!" I say.

He goes to the bathroom and I lie down on my right side. I can still feel the depression in the mattress on his side and move into its warmth. When we were first married I liked that he was a big guy. It felt good, that much bulk in the darkness. I can't remember when his breath started turning bad in the night. Or when I had to turn to face the wall and resented it because, damn, I've got to be friendly to him, even when I am asleep?

He comes back into the bedroom again.

"So anyway, what's your best side for dreams?" I ask him.

He leans over the bed and kisses me. Right up on the hairline where the roots are grey.

He says: "Baby. I don't dream."

Milk and Money

Jane Dugdale

God leaves on Tuesday morning. He picks up his dog collar from the kitchen table and slips out the back door. The cat flap rattles and falls to the floor. The cat doesn't care. It left us weeks ago. Mum's still upstairs in bed, she must be really tired. I tip her corn flakes from her bowl back into the box, loop my tie over my head and sling my rucksack onto my shoulder. It's time for school.

On Wednesday, the milkman's left two bottles of blue top on the front doorstep. It's the first time he's been in three weeks. 'Breakfast's ready,' I shout upstairs, but Mum doesn't shout back. My corn flakes go soggy. They sink to the bottom of my bowl. It's ten past nine. I'm late. I swallow them straight down. Mum's go in the sink and milk trickles from the mushy mound to the plug hole.

Back home on Thursday. Mum's in her flowery nightie, knelt on the kitchen floor. She scrubs and scrubs and scrubs the grey lino, chanting over and over 'stupid dirty floor.' Her hands are shriveled and red. They look really sore. She stands, her nightie's see-through up to her knees. I try not to stare. The bucket's brown water goes down the sink. I don't think she knows I'm there.

'Oi, get back to school,' shouts Mum. She's outside the Post Office with Linda and Lesley. Eyes lined with shades of blue, hair backcombed and stuck up. It's Friday afternoon. She'll be picking up her money before going on to the bingo. She waves at me and her skirt lifts up. Her tights are full of ladders. 'If I win I'll pick up some chips for tea.'

Mum pulls me by the hand, along the high street, to the *Hope and Anchor*. Inside, Dad's sat on a stool with his back straight and head bent back. He's watching the horses on TV. 'Here's your daughter. I want her out of the house. No, she's not got school. It's Saturday you fool.' Dad buys me a half-a-lager shandy. I sit and sip. A horse falls. Dad slumps and knocks back my drink.

At Church, God tells us we're blessed. Mum doesn't seem to agree. She palms the envelopes from the collection bag and whispers, 'Not stealing love. Just taking what's mine. What I'm owed.' In Sunday school they've got pink and yellow party rings, and broken bourbons, on a chipped saucer next to the hot water urn. I tip them into my coat pocket. Nobody notices me.

On Monday, God sits at the kitchen table. Mum says, 'The Reverend's come round for tea.' I pour myself the last glass of milk and go upstairs. In my bedroom, my ginger fur-ball's asleep on my pillow. I sit on the edge of my bed, nibble on a bourbon and stroke the cat. The two pairs of feet on the floorboards outside my room don't bother it, just me.

Startled

Claudia Smith

I was always furious on my mother's behalf. This made it easy for her to take the high road. She was forgiving, gentle. I was difficult, the difficult one, knotting my hair up in ugly little balls on top of my head. Glaring at men and their brutality. He didn't mean it, she always said that. She said all the things the Donahue show said she would say. He didn't mean it. Look what you made him do.

She wore her hair in layered petals, a little cap of petals curling at the nape of her neck.

It was an unspoken understanding between us. I asked for it. She didn't.

Afterwards, he would cry, and he would bring her something. He would hold me, too, against his wet neck. Sometimes, they left me alone to calm down. He would take her places, and when they came home, I'd be waiting in my room, waiting for her to come and say goodnight.

The years went by and his gifts—a flower, a lipstick from the drugstore, a Hallmark card, a fortune cookie, a ripe peach from the farmer's stand—still made her clasp her neck, twist the fake pearls around her fingertips, bite her bottom lip.

I was ugly, hateful, unforgiving. I stayed in my room reading the Farmer's Almanac, the Encyclopedia Britannica, or the bible. We didn't have any other books. I stabbed my tightly wound hair through with pencils or chopsticks. I bit the back of my hand, and felt my teeth, so sharp, like needles. In the other room it went on, a beautiful performance, the man bending down, reaching for her hand, touching her wilted hair with such delicacy. Her eyes were startled, innocent. It was a scene the actors were tired of but wanted to get right, if they could only get it right, if they could just get it right.

Mrs Livingstone's Artist

Kirsty Cowan

Mr Williams was an *artist*, Mrs Livingstone told Mrs Aiken. It was proof, if any were needed, that Mrs Livingstone's boarding house was much more cultured than Mrs Aiken's. Obviously when Mr Williams had been passing he had noticed the careful way her curtains had been tied, the artfully arranged dahlias in the window.

'I wouldn't want an artist staying,' Mrs Aiken said. 'That man looks like he smells.' Mrs Livingstone retorted that he did not, at least not more than men usually did and anyway did it matter? Picasso might have smelt, Rembrandt almost certainly did but they were still great artists. 'Well, I very much doubt he's Picasso,' Mrs Aiken said, sneering. As if Mrs Aiken knew anything about Picasso! Mrs Livingstone stopped listening, instead recalling with pleasure the moment Mr Williams had stepped into her house and asked if a room might be available. So well dressed, it was clear that he was a cultured and artistic young man. In fact he was the sort of young man Mrs Livingstone had once imagined herself marrying. She hadn't of course, she'd married an accountant from Leith, a tedious waste of a man but at least he'd left her the house.

'An artist. I bet he won't pay his rent on time,' Mrs Aiken said sourly.

One day, Mrs Livingstone let herself into Mr Williams's room. There were canvases stacked against a wall and she turned these round one by one. They were nudes, all female; reclining, crouching, lying. It was clear that Mr Williams had a keen eye for detail. Mrs Livingstone went and rearranged the dahlias in her vase afterwards, flustered.

A few weeks later Mr Williams came to her to say that he

couldn't pay his rent that month. He apologised then said, 'Perhaps I could paint your portrait instead?' His eyes looked directly into hers, the steady darkness of his pupils. The boldness of him! That was artistic freedom. Mrs Livingstone considered for a moment before agreeing, her heart fluttering wildly. She should go up to his room and get herself ready, he said.

Mrs Aiken would not do this, she thought as she began to undress. Mrs Aiken would not slip off her skirt in a room rented by a young man, she would not slide her slip over her head, she would not allow her brassiere to tumble heavily to the rug. But then, Mrs Aiken was not a cultured woman! Once Mrs Livingstone had undressed, she laughed to herself, a deep thrill, and turned around one of the canvases against the wall. A landscape. She turned another. A portrait of a woman in a hat and cardigan. A third revealed similar. Where had the other paintings gone?

She felt the draft on her bare spine the moment the door opened. For a second, neither she nor Mr Williams moved. In a mirror above the sink she saw his shocked face, suspended halfway up the wallpaper like a painting in itself.

I Am My Own David Attenborough

Adam Trodd

I am a living natural history programme. An unflinching long-shot of a lioness tearing me up; paws proprietarily either side of my rump, her head undulating up and down as if she is deep-kissing me rather than eating me slowly through my asshole. I do that wild-eyed bovine thing; the skittering hooves in dust, the blowy, clamping valves of a wet, gunmetal snout. Really, I am giving myself to the eroticism of the scene. It is the most intimate thing I have ever known. Death and I are coming simultaneously.

I should love my cancer. It is more a part of me now than any person I have ever known or loved; my lioness. She first appeared on toilet paper like a smeared poppy petal. Curious the things you do. I smelled it, then dropped the bunched wad into the bowl and marvelled at the smoke rings of red ink pluming up through the water like a child's crystal garden experiment. How many more of those should I see before I take it seriously and make an appointment? I picked up the phone at liver-dark brush strokes and a rosary of mucous that spat from the pouting mouth of my sphincter.

'Get up and walk!' this little neighbourhood boy says to me when he sees me sitting in my wheelchair in the front garden, his uplifted arms rigid as wheel spokes and just as thin. He wants to see my exhausted legs jerk like a puppet's.

I laugh. He is like a miniature televangelist. I see him in an angel-white suit, diamante-frosted lapels and a heavy golden crucifix resting on his shirt front.

"Get up and walk, I said!'

No harm is meant. He just wants me to walk.

'I can't, you little lunatic.' I tell him, 'But thanks anyway.'

I throw him enough money for an ice cream. He lowers his arms and frowns, chin to chest, at the coin that pings at his feet. I know he doesn't care about the money. He wants his miracle.

'Okay, we can try again tomorrow,' he says, picking up the coin.

And he actually does come back, every day for weeks until his mother susses what he's at and grabs hold of him, apologising and dragging him away by the hand as if he is a heavy bucket of water that is awkward to tote. I'm sorry to see him go. I call after her that there's no need to take him away.

Now there's nobody to document my demise; I, who lie here like a doomed water buffalo in the sun, with my halo of flies. Who will be around to witness the moment when the lioness reaches my vital organs and I lay my head down, my last breaths blowing bubbles in the mud?

There's No Such Thing as a Fish

Jude Higgins

To repair their relationship, Kevin and Rachel moved from their city flat to a house in the country with a garden. Neither of them were gardeners. By early summer, the lawn was covered with mole hills. Kevin said it was like a plague of boils – a curse upon them. After researching humane mole control, he bought cards that sang 'Happy Birthday' and pushed them into the earth. The noise and vibrations were supposed to drive the moles insane.

When Rachel came into the garden, the batteries on the cards were already running down, and the tinny voice had settled into a melancholic drone.

'That sound would make anything scarper,' she said. She deepened her voice and joined in with the slow chorus – 'Haaaa-pppy birrr-thdaaay tooo yooou.' He had to smile.

'Don't worry about a few mole hills,' she said. 'I'll plant them up with wildflowers and we'll open the garden so the elderly can troop around and admire our inventiveness.'

'You're laughing at me,' Kevin said. But he didn't mind. She'd taken to bringing her iPad to the table at mealtimes and quoting articles from *The New Scientist*. Being teased was far better than hearing about dark energy and how the stars could one day disappear. Perhaps being in the country was doing them some good.

As if they were celebrating a birthday, he prepared her favourite meal – wild Atlantic salmon poached in coconut milk and lime juice with home-made ice cream for afters.

Rachel stayed in the sunny garden, cleared a whole bed of weeds then laid the table to eat outside. But the oven was slow and the ice-cream wouldn't set. By the time he brought out the salmon, resplendent on a plate garlanded with buttered new potatoes and parsley, she was huddled in a thick fleece at the table, her head over the iPad.

'Shall I serve you a piece of fish?' He willed her to look up and admire his cooking but she carried on tapping the screen.

'Listen to what it says on Wiki. *"Technically there's no such thing as a fish. There are many sea creatures, but most are not related to each other. For example, a salmon is more closely related to a camel than it is to a hagfish."*'

Kevin put the fish slice down and wiped his hands on his apron. Behind Rachel, in one of the mole hills, the last of the birthday cards stuttered to a halt. He was sure he could see fresh earth on top of the mound.

National Flash-Fiction Day 2017
Micro-Fiction Competition
Winners:

First Place Winner:
Fifth Grade

Brianna Snow

We learn that there are tubes inside of us with sleeping babies. One day, boys will wake them up. The babies will grow, open our bodies, and fall out. Until then, we'll bleed—a baby's death each month. Ms. Miller sits at her desk in the back of the room while the video plays. We turn to her to see if this is true. She's holding her stomach with both hands. We look down and do the same.

Second Place Winner:

Geology of a Girl

Stephanie Hutton

Ella kept one pebble in her pocket and rubbed it down to sand, running the grains through her fingers. Stones sneaked in through holes in her shoes. Her legs turned to rock. She leant against the sisterhood of brick on the playground and watched girls skip together like lambs. A boulder weighed heavy in her stomach. She curled forwards by habit. Her head filled with the detritus of life.

A new girl started school in May with fire in her eyes. She whispered to Ella with aniseed breath *'lava is liquid rock,'* then took her hand and ran.

Third Place Winner:

As Liquid is Poured

Sherry Morris

I visit far-flung friends who possess a dancing bear and a well-stocked vodka cabinet. We sit around the kitchen table in our coats, watching my breath form clouds. 'At least the shot glasses are chilled,' my friend says. I'm grateful for their hospitality and anticipate the warmth that begins in my belly and spreads outward. We drink to our health, sing melancholy tunes about lavender fog and eat dark bread. I no longer feel the cold. I will stay here. I won't be missed there. There, people are replaced like vodka bottles. The bear twirls on hind legs and claps.

Highly Commended Stories:

Brave
Catherine Edmunds

The man arrives in a car with dark windows. Father, who is brave, stands in the yard while the pigs squeal and run. The man pushes Father's shoulder. The cockerel struts, the man raises his hand. Father shrinks.

I gather the others and we run down the stinking lane; I tell them Father's play-acting, he'll kill the man later. They like that. They've seen Father cut a squealer's throat. I lead them away down to the mill race, into danger, but it's just water, full of noise. Try to pick it up and it slips through your fingers.

Mermaids

Sally Syson

The mermaids are much uglier than anyone had anticipated, slimy-haired and scabby with barnacles. They haul themselves up onto the sea wall, stinking like a barrel of prawns, and lie flashing their tits at passers-by. They snatch at the ankles of the small boys who dare to pelt them with chips and cans. Their language is appalling.

On Friday nights, when the promenade glistens with broken glass and the splintered remains of cocktail charms — pretty plastic mermaids in pink and green and blue — they retreat to the shoreline and gather along the water's edge, hissing in the dark.

Fireflies in the Backyard

Kayla Pongrac

In the summertime, when these little roving lanterns covet my backyard, slicing their way through the darkness one flight at a time, I step outside and I extend my tongue, snowflake-style, so that I can jar and lid them inside my stomach. How I want to glow, too—how I want to become both the illuminated and the illuminator.

Fawn

Sacha Waldron

Taking the fawn had not been her initial intention. She was feeding it saltines from the palm of her hand, stroking his soft head. She liked the way his tongue felt on her skin. She was, she realised, running out of crackers and soon the deer would scamper off. Its run reminded her of a carousel – rising and falling.

She crouched down, opened her backpack and scattered some of the remaining crumbs inside. The fawn followed them. She zipped up her bag quickly. As she walked out of the park she could feel little hooves sticking awkwardly into her spine.

Mango

Jennifer Harvey

Johnny tells me I'm sweeter than mango. He's standing with his back against the wall, one foot up against the brickwork, like some fifties rebel.

Yeah? You like exotic fruit, Johnny? If I had the guts, I'd say this. Walk on by all sassy, like I owned him. Meet his gaze and wait for a reply.

Your move, Johnny.

But he made his move already. Watched me sat in the canteen, licking mango juice from my fingers.

One finger, two fingers, three fingers, four.

Smiling, 'cos he knew it was him I was thinking of.

The In-Between Hour

Christina Taylor

While you sleep I'll kiss all the boys I shouldn't kiss and wear dresses that scream 'You're not going out in that!'

I'll learn another language so I can talk about you behind your back. I'll dye my hair blue then sneak out of the house to release the dogs. We'll bark at the moon and set off car alarms.

In that hour I'll skinny dip in the river and count the goose bumps on my arms. I'll fly round the sun and eat cake for breakfast.

I'll do all that but I'll never say I love you.

The Smoking Circle

Alison Wassell

We lay in a circle on the field every afternoon, our heads together, school bags for pillows. She was the new girl, refusing to light up until we called her Goody Two Shoes. We stared at the clouds.

'What would you do if you only had a week to live?' someone asked. She answered first.

'I'd write to everyone who'd hurt me. Tell them what I thought of them.'

She was the one who developed a forty a day habit. The letter came sealed with a lipstick kiss. I suppose we all got one. I shredded mine without reading it.

Author Information

We don't have enough room in a volume such as this to list a full biography for all of our authors, and anyway, we don't have to when they have all already done the job for us on their blogs and websites.

So, below, please find a list of the places on the World-Wide Web where you can follow up the authors from this anthology (where available). Please read their other work, buy their books, and generally support them. That way they can continue to bring you wonderful stories like the ones you've just read.

Adam Trodd	@A_Trodd
Alison Wassell	@lilysslave
Angela Readman	@angelreadman
Anna Nazarova-Evans	@AnitchkaNE
Anne Summerfield	@summerwriter
Bobbie Ann Mason	www.bobbieannmason.net
Brianna Snow	@bpaigesnow
Calum Kerr	www.calumkerr.co.uk
Catherine Edmunds	@cathyedmunds
Christina Taylor	@Chrissie72
Christopher M Drew	@cmdrew81
Claire Polders	www.clairepolders.com
Claudia Smith	www.claudiastories.com
Conor Houghton	@conorjh
Danielle McLaughlin	www.daniellemclaughlin.ie
David O'Neill	@cartoonmoonirl
David Steward	@DavidSteward7
Diane Simmons	dianesimmons.wixsite.com/dianesimmons
Erica Plouffe Lazure	ericaplouffelazure.com
Etgar Keret	etgarkeret.com
Gary Duncan	spelkfiction.com
Gary V. Powell	www.authorgaryvpowell.com
Gay Degani	www.gaydegani.com
Heather McQuillan	heathermcquillan.wordpress.com
Helen Rye	@helenrye
Ingrid Jendrzejewski	www.ingridj.com
James Coffey	jamesvcoffey@aol.com
Jane Dugdale	@janeannedugdale
Jason Jackson	www.jjfiction.wordpress.com
Jennifer Harvey	www.jenharvey.net
Joanna Campbell	joanna-campbell.com

Jonathan Taylor	www.jonathanptaylor.co.uk
Joy Manné	www.joymanne.org
Jude Higgins	@judehwriter
Judi Walsh	@judi_walsh
Judy Darley	www.SkyLightRain.com
Kayla Pongrac	www.kaylapongrac.com
Kevlin Henney	semantic.net
Kirsty Cowan	@thiskirstycowan
KM Elkes	kmelkes.co.uk
Lex Williford	www.lexwilliford.com
Lindsay Fisher	fishpie3@hotmail.com
Marie Gethins	@MarieGethins
Mark Connors	www.markconnors.co.uk
Mary Lynn Reed	marylynnreed.com
Matthew Thorpe-Coles	@mattisacoles
Meg Pokrass	megpokrass.com
Megan Crosbie	www.mcrosbie.com
Michael Loveday	www.michaelloveday.co.uk
Miranda Kate	purplequeennl.blogspot.nl
Nod Ghosh	www.nodghosh.com/about
Nuala Ní Chonchúir	www.nualanichonchuir.com
Paul Currion	www.currion.net
Peter Wortsman	www.facebook.com/peter.wortsman
Rachael Dunlop	@RachaelDunlop
Robert Lopez	blpress.org/books/good-people
Rupert Dastur	@RupertDastur
Sacha Waldron	sachawaldron.contently.com
Sally Syson	@sallysyson
Sandra Arnold	@sandra32857098
Santino Prinzi	www.tinoprinzi.wordpress.com
Sharon Telfer	@sharontelfer
Sherry Morris	www.uksherka.com
Simon Sylvester	www.simonsylvester.wordpress.com
Sophia Holme	quinklings.wordpress.com
Sophie Rosenblum	www.sophierosenblum.com
Sophie van Llewyn	@sophie_van_l
Stephanie Hutton	www.stephaniehutton.com
Stephen Tuffin	stephentuffin2017.wordpress.com
Steven Moss	www.stevenrmoss.co.uk
Tim Stevenson	www.timjstevenson.com
Victoria Richards	www.victoriarichards.co.uk
Zoe Murdock	www.facebook.com/zoemurdockauthor

Note: the @names are for Twitter profiles.

Acknowledgements

First, thanks to the judges of the micro-fiction competition: Kevlin Henney, Ingrid Jendrzejewski, Anne Patterson, Angela Readman, Tim Stevenson, and Rob Walton. Reading through the many entries we receive and selecting the winners requires a lot of time, energy, and deliberation. Congratulations, once again, to the winners.

Special thanks must go to my co-editor, Meg Pokrass, for helping me with the difficult but enjoyable task of reading through all of the anthology submissions. Her invaluable insight has helped to make this anthology truly mesmerising.

Thanks to Helen Rye for allowing us to borrow her enchanting title for the anthology.

Thank you to our proof-readers who have done a wonderful job ironing out the creases.

To all of the authors who shared with us their stories: thank you. Without your words, these pages would be empty.

Thanks again to Tim Stevenson, who keeps the website alive.

Special thanks to Calum Kerr for his advice and support, his wisdom, belief, and for NFFD itself. The gratitude and appreciation I have for you knows no bounds.

- Santino Prinzi

Also Available from National Flash-Fiction Day

A Box of Stars Beneath the Bed (NFFD 2016)

No theme, just great stories. Authors include: Sarah Hilary, Angela Readman, Claire Fuller, Paul McVeigh, Santino Prinzi, Nik Perring, Meg Pokrass, Michelle Elvy, Tim Stevenson, Debbie Young, Kevlin Henney, Nuala Ní Chonchúir and NFFD Director, Calum Kerr.

Landmarks (NFFD 2015)

Geographical stories that take you places. Authors include: Sarah Hilary, Angela Readman, SJI Holliday, Nik Perring, Michelle Elvy, Tim Stevenson, Jonathan Pinnock, Nuala Ní Chonchúir and Calum Kerr.

Eating My Words (NFFD 2014)

Stories of the senses. Authors include Michael Marshall Smith, Sarah Hillary, Angela Readman, Calum Kerr, Nuala Ní Chonchúir, Nik Perring, Nigel McLoughlin, Cathy Bryant, Tim Stevenson, Tania Hershman and Jon Pinnock.

Scraps
(NFFD 2013)

Stories inspired by other artworks. Authors include Jenn Ashworth, Cathy Bryant, Vanessa Gebbie, David Hartley, Kevlin Henney, Tania Hershman, Sarah Hilary, Holly Howitt, Calum Kerr, Emma J. Lannie, Stephen McGeagh, Jonathan Pinnock, Dan Powell, Tim Stevenson, and Alison Wells.

Jawbreakers
(NFFD 2012)

One-word titles only! Includes stories from Ian Rankin, Vanessa Gebbie, Jenn Ashworth, Tania Hershman, David Gaffney, Trevor Byrne, Jen Campbell, Jonathan Pinnock, Calum Kerr, Valerie O'Riordan and many more.

Other books from **Gumbo Press**:
www.gumbopress.co.uk

On Cleanliness and Other Stories
by Tim Stevenson

Thirteen stories that journey between the gothic past and the very far future: where a washing machine arrives unannounced to change the course of a life, and the colours at the end of the world are our oldest enemy. Discover why the mushrooms in the cellar bite back, how a little girl's birthday present can have a life of its own, and why, in the wrong hands, imaginary guns can still be very, very dangerous.

28 Far Cries by Marc Nash

This latest collection of flash-fictions from Marc Nash. The stories range from the violence of Happy Hour to armoured pole-dancers, from dying superheroes to synesthesia, and from toxic relationships to warlords to the mythic ponderings of incubi and succubi. Each flash-fiction is crafted with Nash's usual close attention to detail and the nuances of language, to captivate and intrigue.

Rapture and what comes after
by Virginia Moffatt

For every tale of everlasting love... You'll find another full of heartbreak and misery. Where other love stories end with the coming of the light, Virginia Moffatt goes beyond to show the darkness which can exist in even the happiest relationships. These stories are by turns funny, sad, heart-warming and heart-breaking.

The Book of Small Changes
by Tim Stevenson

This collection takes its inspiration from the Chinese I Ching: where the sea mourns for those it has lost, encyclopaedia sales-men weave their accidental magic, and the only true gift for a king is the silence of snow.

Enough by Valerie O'Riordan

Fake mermaids and conjoined twins, Johannes Gutenberg, airplane sex, anti-terrorism agricultural advice, Bluebeard and more. Ten flash-fictions.

Threshold by David Hartley

Threshold explores the surreal and the strange through thirteen flash-fictions which take us from a neighbour's garden, out into space, and even as far as Preston. But which Preston?

Undead at Heart by Calum Kerr

War of the Worlds meets *The Walking Dead* in this novel from Calum Kerr, author of *31* and *Braking Distance*.

The World in a Flash: How to Write Flash-Fiction by Calum Kerr

A guide for beginners and experienced writers alike to give you insight into the world of flash-fiction. Chapters focus on a range of aspects, with exercises for you to try.

The 2014 Flash365 Collections
by Calum Kerr

Apocalypse

It's the end of the world as we know it. Fire is raining from the sky, monsters are rising from the deep, and the human race is caught in the middle.

The Audacious Adventuress

Our intrepid heroine, Lucy Burkhampton, is orphaned and swindled by her evil nemesis, Lord Diehardt. She must seek a way to prove her right to her family's wealth, to defeat her enemy, and more than anything, to stay alive.

The Grandmaster
Unrelated strangers are being murdered in a brutal fashion. Now it's up to crime-scene cleaner Mike Chambers, with the help of the police, to track down the killer and stop the trail of carnage.

Lunch Hour
One office. Many lives. It is that time of day: the time for poorly-filled, pre-packaged sandwiches; the time to run errands you won't have enough time for; the time to fall in love, to kill or be killed, to take advice from an alien. It's the Lunch Hour.

Time
Time. It's running out. It's flying. It's the most precious thing, and yet it never slows, never stops, never waits. In this collection we visit the past, the future, and sometimes a present we no longer recognise. And it's all about time.

In Conversation with Bob and Jim
Bob and Jim have been friends for forty years, but still have plenty to say to each other - usually accompanied by a libation or two. This collections shines a light on an enduring relationship, the ups and downs, and the prospect of oncoming mortality. It is funny and poignant, and entirely told in dialogue.

Saga
One Family. Seven Generations.
Spanning 1865 to 2014, *Saga* follows a single family as it grows and changes. Stories cover war and peace, birth and death, love and loss, are all set against a background of change. More than anything, however, these are stories of people and of family.

Strange is the New Black
Spaceships and aliens, alternative histories and parallel universes, robots, computers, faraway worlds, run-away science and the end of the world; all these and more are the province of science-fiction, and all these and more can be found in this new collection.

The Ultimate Quest

Our heroine Lucy Burkhampton, swindled heiress and traveller through the worlds of literature, is now jumping from genre to genre in search of a mythical figure known only as The Author. Can she reach the real world? Can she escape the deadly clutches of her enemy? Can she finally reclaim her family name?

There's only one way to find out.

Read on...

Christmas

Jeff and Maddie are hosting Christmas this year, for their two boys - Ethan and Jake - for her parents, his father, his brother James and partner Gemma, and for a surprise guest. It's a time of peace and joy, but how long can that last when a family comes together?

Graduation Day

It's Graduation Day, a time for celebration, but for a group of students, their family and their friends, it is going to be a day of terror as the whole ceremony is taken hostage. In the audience sits the target of the terrorists' intentions: Senator Eleanor Thornton. But not far away from her is a man who might just make a difference: former-FBI Agent Jim Sikorski. Can he foil their plans and save the hostages, or will terror rule the day?

Post Apocalypse

Fire fell from the skies, the dead rose from the ground, and aliens watched from orbit as the Great Old Ones enslaved the human race. That was the Apocalypse. This is what happened next. Brandon returns, in thrall, and Todd continues his worship. Jackson finds unconventional ways to fight back, and General Xorle-Jian-Splein takes new control of his mission. The world has ended, but in these 31 flash-fictions, the story continues.

The 2014 Flash365 Anthology

12 Books 365 New Flash-Fictions All in one volume. This book contains: Apocalypse The Audacious Adventuress The Grandmaster Lunch Hour Time In Conversation with Bob and Jim Saga Strange is the New Black The Ultimate Quest Christmas Graduation Day Post Apocalypse 12 books full of tiny stories crossing and mixing genres: crime, science-fiction, horror, stream-of-consciousness, surrealism, comedy, romance, realism, adventure and more. From the end of the world to the start of a life; families being happy and families in trouble; travelling in time and staying in the moment, this volume brings you every kind of story told in every kind of way.

Printed in Great Britain
by Amazon